MOUNTAINBOARD MANIACS

take it to the Xtreme

MOUNTAINBOARD MANIACS

Pam Withers

Walrus Books
A Division of Whitecap Books Ltd.

Edited by Carolyn Bateman
Proofread by Joan E. Templeton
Cover and interior design by Roberta Batchelor
Cover photograph of Casey Thomas © Ground Industries Inc.
Typeset by Setareh Ashrafologhalai

Printed and bound in Canada

Library and Archives Canada Cataloguing in Publication

Withers, Pam
Mountainboard maniacs / Pam Withers.

(Take it to the extreme ; #10)
ISBN 978-1-55285-915-5

I. Title. II. Series: Withers, Pam. Take it to the extreme ; #10.

PS8595.I8453M69 2008 jC813'.6 C2007-905174-X

The publisher acknowledges the financial support of the Canada Council for the Arts, the British Columbia Arts Council, and the Government of Canada through the Book Publishing Industry Development Program (BPIDP). Whitecap Books also acknowledges the financial support of the Province of British Columbia through the Book Publishing Tax Credit.

Canada Council for the Arts   Conseil des Arts du Canada

The inside pages of this book are 100% recycled, processed chlorine-free paper with 40% post-consumer content. For more information, visit Markets Initiative's website: www.oldgrowthfree.com.

ANCIENT FOREST FRIENDLY

As the tenth and final book in the Take It to the Xtreme series, *Mountainboard Maniacs* can be dedicated to only one person: Carolyn Bateman, my editor throughout. She has done more to "grow" me as a writer than anyone. Thanks, Carolyn, for your patience and talent.

Contents

Prologue

A Short History of Mount St. Helens's 1980 Eruption

There are about six hundred potentially active volcanoes in the world, not counting those hidden under the seas. Close to fifty of these erupt each year, most too remote to make the news.

Before 1980, Mount St. Helens (between Seattle, Washington, and Portland, Oregon) had been dormant for more than a century. When it first showed signs of waking up, the state governor declared everything within five miles of the peak a "Red Zone"—off limits to everyone but scientists and law-enforcement officials.

Just six miles north of the peak, an observation post manned by a thirty-year-old scientist named David Johnston was considered safe. Yet when Mount St. Helens erupted violently on May 18, 1980, it killed fifty-seven people, including Johnston—instantly vaporizing his body, jeep, camper, and nearby trees after he'd radioed colleagues, "This is it …"

First, a 5.1-magnitude earthquake shook the ground. Seconds later, the mountain's north flank collapsed, producing the largest debris avalanche in living history. Moving at nearly 180 miles per hour, the avalanche turned a huge area into a moon-like landscape.

The avalanche "uncorked" the volcano, which blasted rock, ash, and hot gases downhill at supersonic speeds of up to 670 miles per hour. The deadly blast was five hundred times greater than that of the Hiroshima atomic bomb.

A young man and his girlfriend well outside the Red Zone saw the blast cloud coming at their camping site. They clung to each other as trees crashed all around and, even though they were nearly buried by ash, they managed to stay alive. Two friends only a short distance away died when their tent was crushed.

Shortly after the first blast, St. Helens unleashed a stronger explosion accompanied by a column of ash that rose more than twenty miles in less than ten minutes and expanded into a mushroom-shaped cloud. Near the volcano, swirling ash particles in the atmosphere triggered lightning strikes, which in turn ignited forest fires. In some areas, the cloud was so dense it turned day into night.

The blast's heat melted the mountain's snowcap, forcing hot mudflows to cascade for dozens of miles down the mountain's river valleys. Flowing like wet cement, these mudflows killed at least three people when they overran two logging camps twelve miles below the volcano's former peak.

Twenty-three miles below the summit, a couple camping along the Toutle River barely escaped death when a mudflow swept them up and carried them for almost a mile before they were able to wade to shore. In some places, mudflows were hundreds of feet deep, leaving "bathtub rings" on valley walls.

In an amazing finale, at least seventeen pyroclastic (fragmented lava) flows rushed down the mountain, covering the debris already deposited by avalanches and mudflows. As a result, some debris remained hot even two weeks after the disaster.

By the end of the nine-hour eruption, gray humps of congealed mud and debris had replaced all the lush forest within eight miles of the mountain's collapsed top. Even nineteen miles from the smoking crater, only fallen trees that resembled broken matchsticks remained. And beyond that? For many miles, only dead, scorched trees stood, killed by the hot gases of the blast.

During the first few days after the eruption, as ash drifted all the way to Oklahoma, rescuers moved in to save nearly two hundred survivors.

Only time and nature can make the landscape

green and the mountain serene again. In fact, Mount St. Helens will take centuries to mend entirely, assuming it experiences no further violent eruptions. Yet the speedy resurgence of life has been one of the eruption's most valuable lessons. That, and the reminder that volcanoes do not always behave in predictable or logical ways. The unexpected sometimes does happen.

Adapted with permission from The Volcano Adventure Guide *by Rosaly Lopes (Cambridge University Press, 2005).*

1 Exam

White chalk screeching against a blackboard at the front of a dead-quiet classroom. A beam of brilliant sunlight bursting through dark, heavy clouds outside. That's what Jake Evans would remember about the moments leading up to the chaos that brought about the first stage of his downfall. It was the calm before the storm, even though the thunder and rain had only just stopped. Jake could smell the chalk from where he sat. As it squeaked against the board, it trickled flecks as dry and powdery as fine ash; it made his nose tickle. His usual teachers used the whiteboard.

He was sitting in an aisle desk near the front of the classroom at his school in Chilliwack, British Columbia. The aisle position gave him a slight advantage for what was about to unfold. He'd only glanced out the window at the cloud break for a second. He was concentrating very hard on Nancy Sheppard's chalk. It was forming the words "final exam," and he was feeling pumped. He knew he was going to ace the test; all the students knew he was going to. He wasn't cocky about being this class's top dog, or about being the teacher's pet. That wasn't part of his personality.

It's not as if he was a brain in any other classes. It's just that at that particular moment—sitting there watching the word "final exam" take form—he was calm, primed, and wrapped in confidence. The pride before the fall, his mother would say.

Then the chalk fell from Nancy's hand, her mouth opened wide, and out came that word, the one that rattled Jake's confidence.

"Explosion!"

For a split-second, everyone just sat dumbly at their desks, staring at their teacher as she waved her arms wildly at the door.

"Get out!" Nancy shouted louder, eyes wide. "File out to the parking lot, now!"

Jake felt a bolt of adrenalin lift him out of his desk and hurl him down the aisle toward the door at the back of the room. Soon a dozen other students were stampeding behind him in the same direction, screaming, pushing, jostling, crushing one another in their race to be first out of the building. Jake's fast reaction time put him at the head of the pack. Years of doing extreme sports gave him that advantage.

He looked left, right. Nothing but the empty, potholed gravel schoolyard, still damp from the rain shower. Then he looked twenty-five yards ahead at the parking lot and drew in his breath. He counted six bodies sprawled in unnatural poses on the dark, steamy tarmac. Only one was moving: a skinny, red-soaked figure dragging its lower body with the help of ragged jerks from its twisted upper body. Jake powered his long legs into an all-out sprint. Just as he reached the disaster scene, the crawling student—a boy he knew—collapsed into a stunned heap.

"Stay calm," Jake told himself as he drew near. "Just figure out who needs help first."

He stopped and squatted beside the closest student, a girl lying on her back, as the crowd behind him caught up and ran to other victims. Her eyes were closed and her face was as white as Nancy's chalk. He could see no wounds or obvious injuries, yet when he bent his ear over her mouth, he could feel no breath. Quickly, his fingers reached for the place on her neck where he'd feel her pulse.

"Nothing," he muttered soberly to a boy kneeled nearby who was going through the same motions on another still body.

"Same," the boy said solemnly, eyes large.

"Leave them," Jake ruled, springing up and glancing about, trying to take in the whole scene at once.

"You sure?" his classmate asked, looking hesitantly from the body he'd just declared dead, to the girl's body, to Jake.

"Yes!" Jake shouted, already on his way to the figure that had stopped crawling seconds before. "They're dead, Todd! Nothing we can do for them!" What kind of explosion had it been, anyway?

The guy who had been crawling only seconds before was definitely bleeding, Jake realized as he took a deep, steadying breath. Plus his hair looked as if it had been combed from the ends to the roots. His face and T-shirt were scorched black where they weren't stained red. Worse, where portions of his shirt had been burned away, the skin beneath was an even more shocking red. The boy had every right to be screaming, but he was barely whimpering as he lay on the wet blacktop, shivering and trying to focus on the crowd around him.

"He's burned," Jake declared as his mind raced through everything he'd read on what to do with burn victims. A circle of faces turned up to Jake expectantly. Nancy was nowhere in sight.

"Cover the burns with clean dressings. Don't touch them or they'll get infected. Give him a drink of water and watch he doesn't go into shock before the ambulance gets here," Jake said. "He should be first into the ambulance."

"How will we know if he starts to go into shock?"

one of the onlookers asked another, but before anyone could answer, a high-pitched shriek sounded from the far end of the parking lot.

Jake recognized the voice as the scream traveled like a knife tip from his eardrum to his brain. His feet flew toward the sound of his best friend, Peter Montpetit.

"This one's got several broken bones," a girl called from his left. Jake turned his head, saw she was referring to a boy who was blinking and moaning. Jake slowed, but his feet refused to change direction. He thought he could see Peter sitting up, swaying from side to side, one hand clutching a shoulder as if it was about to fall off.

"Is he conscious, Lila?" Jake asked the girl. His head swiveled toward her but his body was already a few paces past her.

"Yeah—barely," Lila replied, a tremor in her voice. "What do I do?"

"Leave him for later. Go help with the burned guy," Jake snapped, pouring on speed as Peter's cries went hysterical.

Peter's screeches were singeing Jake's nerves. He knew he wouldn't be able to focus on anyone else until he calmed his friend down. Peter never, ever screamed. Jake should know. The two had grown up together, and they were both into sports and adventure. They had tried almost every extreme sport around. Their mothers liked to joke they'd used up all their nine lives long ago.

Their latest fanaticism was mountainboarding: careening down hills at up to sixty miles per hour on what looked like a snowboard on wheels. They considered the scrapes and bruises no big deal. Jake and Peter loved living life to the extreme.

But hollering like a banshee? Never. Jake's legs felt as hollow as his throat by the time he reached Peter.

He tallied up the disaster scene's casualties. Two dead, one badly burned, one with broken bones but conscious. And Peter, who sounded pretty bad. Where was Nancy? Wait. There had been six bodies. Jake did a quick side glance to check out the last figure: a girl being helped to her feet near Peter. She looked like a poster child for road rash: seriously bloody scrapes and bruises all over. But the kid was talking to her helpers, a good sign.

"Anything broken? How bad are the cuts?" Jake gestured impatiently to the kids around the standing girl while he still made a beeline for Peter.

"Nope. Lots of scrapes, but nothing deep," someone answered.

"Then leave her. Help me with Peter here, or go help the burned guy," he suggested.

They nodded and began moving away from the girl, even as her sobs increased.

Jake placed a trembling hand on the shoulder of his blond, curly-haired friend. "Peter, what's wrong?"

"Noooo!" Peter screeched, batting Jake's hand away as if he'd just stuck a finger into a deep wound. Then his eyes rolled back in their sockets and he wavered as if about to pass out. His screams turned to sobs.

"Peter! Is something broken? What's going on?" Jake half-expected to see a bone end sticking right out of Peter's shoulder and a geyser of blood. Jake had never, ever seen Peter cry. Peter could suck it up better than anyone he knew.

"What's with him?" a girl asked. "We've been trying to help him, but he won't let us near him."

"Peter, you have to tell me what's wrong, or at least quiet down. I'm going to check you over."

Peter's sobs turned to gasps as Jake lifted his shirt. Nothing. No blood, burns, or scratches. Still, might be internal bleeding. Something that could put Peter into shock any second. People can die when they go into shock. That much Jake knew.

Unlike most of his classmates, he'd had lots of first-aid training. As a junior outdoor guide for the local outfitter, Sam's Adventure Tours, he was required to have that kind of stuff under his belt. And he'd used it, more than once. So had Peter, a junior guide with Sam's company, too.

Jake knew his training meant he shouldn't be feeling

rattled here in a school parking lot after some kind of explosion—even if two people were dead and Peter was badly injured. But he was rattled, Jake realized as Peter's eyes rolled again.

"Make sure he's the second one into the ambulance," Jake pronounced. But none of the students around replied. They were studying someone behind him.

Jake looked up to see Nancy standing over him, shaking her head. Her dark eyes fixed on him, revealing a level of disappointment he'd never seen before. His heart sank even before she spoke.

"The boy with the multiple fractures has died," she told him solemnly. "He went into shock right after you passed him to help Peter. He and the burn victim should have been your top priorities. Peter has nothing but a dislocated shoulder and an overactive set of lungs, isn't that right, Peter?"

Peter grinned as the six supposed victims of the pretend explosion jumped up and wandered over. "That's right, and I'm the best actor in this first-aid class, right? Sorry about psyching you out, Jake old buddy, but nice to know you care." Peter punched Jake's shoulder playfully.

Jake felt like punching him back, hard enough to give him a real dislocated shoulder. His bellowing had thrown Jake off. But it wasn't Peter's fault that Nancy was giving Jake a withering gaze while making notes on her clipboard. Jake had flunked, he knew. Flunked his final exam on this Saturday first-aid course—right in front of schoolmates at his own school. But far worse, he'd let down Nancy, who also happened to be the manager at Sam's Adventure Tours.

"Sorry, Jake," Nancy was saying. "Where you went wrong was ignoring the girl who told you that the broken-bones victim was only barely conscious. That meant he could go into shock. Remember, the level of pain someone seems to have does not always indicate what level of danger they are in. And we must never let favoritism for friends get in the way of a professional assessment in triage."

Triage, this class had learned, was coping with a disaster scene by dividing victims into three categories: the dead (beyond help), the ones needing immediate help, and the "walking wounded," or those who could wait. For this final exam, Nancy had arranged for six students to play-act two victims, complete with realistic makeup, in each of the three categories. Jake, playing the medical team's leader for this exam, was supposed to make sure his helpers left the dead and walking wounded until after they'd dealt with the more serious cases.

"I understand," Jake said, hanging his head and refusing to meet Peter's taunting eyes. "You're right. Do I have to take the whole course over again?"

"I'm afraid so," Nancy said, nodding sympathetically and resting her hand on his shoulder. "But there's still time to do that and renew your qualification before the mountainboarding trip in Washington state."

"Yes!" Peter enthused, punching a fist into the open palm of his other hand.

"No way—luck-ee," a couple of kids murmured around them.

"You two're getting paid to go mountainboarding somewhere?" the burn victim asked.

Jake allowed a smile back onto his face. "Yup. That's what outdoor guides do. Hey, how did you get those burns to look so gross?"

The boy grinned and slid an arm around the shoulders of the white-faced girl who'd been holding her breath when Jake had positioned his ear over her mouth. She'd also whispered "no pulse" when he'd tried to get a pulse on her.

"Charcoal on the face," he informed everyone as he touched his face, "and my girlfriend's lipstick on my chest."

That sent hooting and ripples of laughter through the crowd as his girlfriend blushed just enough to show color through her chalk-rubbed face. "I guess this shirt is toast now," the boy added, "what with the ketchup stains and the fun I had last night with a cigarette lighter."

Jake tried to smile, even though he was feeling totally bummed out. A flunkee. That's what he was.

"Okay, gang," Nancy said, lowering her clipboard and tossing her long, dark hair over her shoulders. "Back to the classroom to trade places for the next triage test. A different disaster this time."

I'll pass this course next time, Jake promised himself as he watched black clouds outnumber white clouds once more. I won't disappoint Nancy again. He told himself that, but his heart felt heavy. His confidence seemed to have gone into hiding like the sun. He shivered and followed the kids back to the school building.

"I'm playing a victim next round," Jake said to no one in particular, jamming his unruly brown hair into his baseball cap. "Pass the ketchup."

2 Air and Water

Jake was rolling his mountainboard backwards and forwards at the top of a gentle grassy rise leading smoothly down into a kicker anchored to the ground with tent pegs. The homemade kicker was a quarter-pipe with a curved lower end designed to shoot you into the air. He could smell the burgers on the deck of the restaurant just behind him. He could hear the tinkle of glasses from the diners likely watching him and hoping for a dramatic spill to spice their meal. He could also hear the cheers and jeers of the young mountainboarders lined up behind him.

"Hurry it up! Doesn't take that long to set up."

"Go Jake. You show 'em how it's done!" That last voice was Nancy's. His own personal cheerleader. His thirty-year-old boss. Someone who always believed in him, good times or bad. He owed lots to her. So much that it sometimes felt like a weight on his shoulders.

He looked down and rubbed his neck for a second, like the weight was real. But he did want to show the little kids behind him how it was done.

"Come on!" Peter shouted. "Let 'er rip!"

Just time to take one deep breath and push off. His mountainboard rolled down the rise and tore toward the kicker before carving an arc up into the sky. With his feet tight in the bindings, he leaned back and pulled a fast double backflip like an airplane skywriting two e's. Up, up until he was hanging from the sky by his feet and board, blood rushing to his head. Two full flips like that and then down, down until he was dropping out of the sky, board first. His arms spread instinctively like wings to hold his balance. If he'd been riding a dirt jump, he'd have landed it as smoothly as a practiced airplane pilot. But on this hot summer day, there was just the clear, cool river below him. Splashdown! The mountainboard's flat bottom—its deck—splashed big as he bombed purposefully into the water. He sank in slow motion, like an actor being lowered down a trapdoor mid-stage—arms raised, cheers from the audience roaring its approval.

Then the water muted the noise. Clingy bubbles tickled his body and pushed themselves up his nose as his lifejacket slowed him to a stop. Anxious not to risk the next trickster landing on his head, he plunged his hands down to release his feet from his board, then shot to the surface with it and stroked to the river dock. The crowd was still cheering as he handed his board up to Peter. He lifted and rolled his body onto the dock's damp boards.

"Nice double," Peter said approvingly, slapping him on the back of his life jacket while pocketing a book he'd been reading on the dock. "We'll show these little brats we're the bosses, hey?"

"Something like that," Jake said with a grin, shaking water from his hair as he lifted his helmet off.

He and Peter had decided that mountainboarding was the best free-ride adventure sport around. Operating on ten-inch tires, the boards weighed nearly fourteen pounds, required lots of body armor, and cost maybe triple what a skateboard did. Because it was a relatively new sport, the boys weren't as good at it as they were at other sports. But they were getting better quickly, and they hoped their boss Sam Miller had noticed. He'd been saying how important it was that his guides were aces at the sport. He'd also been going on about trying to attract more female clients, which was cool with the boys, especially girl-crazy Peter.

"Did someone say 'little brats'?" Nancy asked, chuckling as she handed Jake his towel. "Now, now, careful how you talk about potential sign-ups for our trips. You're doing a good job of impressing their parents. See that lineup of adults at the sign-up table?"

Jake glanced at the table set up on the park's green, grassy lawn between the kicker and the restaurant entrance. They were in a pleasant suburb of Seattle with a view of fog-shrouded, snow-capped Mount Rainier forming an impressive backdrop. A line of adults stood chatting as their kids on demo boards flattened the grass in wobbly circles before tipping over and giggling up at their friends.

"Looks good," Jake said. He could hardly wait to guide a pack of kids down the Northwest's rugged mountain slopes. Although first, there'd be the guides-only training trips to get familiar with the trails.

"Looks very good," Nancy said. "Lots of girl signups, too. That'll make Sam happy. He sure has been pushing for that. Hey, have you boys eaten lunch yet? Lunch is free for Sam's Adventure Tours staff, you know."

"No, boss, we haven't!" Peter said. "Been too busy flying off the kicker. Did you see my Superman? Perfect day for jumping in a river. Best way for all these kids to get big air and try out new tricks without 'wearing' their falls. Good thing the sealed bearings on all these boards are stainless steel so the water doesn't hurt them. Yeah, let's all go eat!"

Jake, amused as always by Peter's motor-mouthing, nodded as he toweled down. Nancy bent down to pick up the clipboard she was always carrying and walked up the riverbank with them.

They seated themselves at the restaurant's deck. In the center of the table sat a plate loaded with giant slices of juicy-looking red watermelon. Their plates loaded with burgers, fries, and salad, the three had a perfect view of the action below.

"The kids are having a blast!" Peter enthused between bites of burger as the cheers and splashes drowned out much of the conversation around them. "Bet you they all sign up!"

Jake peeked at the book Peter had set beside him on the table and grinned: *Volcano Survival Stories*. Just because they'd be mountainboarding down some inactive volcanoes around here, Peter had to read stuff that would make his imagination work overtime.

Nancy was scribbling on her clipboard between absent-minded forkfuls of salad. "Mountainboarding is one of the fastest-growing sports around."

"That's 'cause pretty much anyone can do it," Jake pointed out. "Once you've got a board, it's not like you have to pay for lift tickets or queue for space at a skateboard park. All you need is a hill and a kicker to pull off whatever freestyle moves you want."

Jake, like Peter, could appreciate a cool new sport that took boarding to new places. Then again, he and Peter hadn't had to pay for their boards, thanks to their jobs doing adventure tours.

"And the kids who've done skateboarding or snowboarding or wakeboarding or surfing ace it pretty quickly," Peter added. "The moms and dads here are loving the demo day. Smart thinking, Nancy. You really know how to grow this business, don't you?"

Whoa, Jake thought. That's really sucking up to her. Peter had been doing a lot of that lately.

"Mmmm," Nancy replied, pencil paused above her clipboard. "Peter, when's your birthday?"

"Glad you asked! It's July 20th, just a couple of weeks away. And chocolate cake with fudge frosting is my favorite."

Jake shook his head with a half-smile as Nancy continued.

"Okay, and how long have you been with Sam's Adventure Tours?"

"I joined a year after Jake did," Peter said. "Summer of—"

"I know when Jake joined," Nancy interrupted him, head lifting to smile at Jake. She put her pencil down. "Seems like a long time ago. You were the hardest working kid we'd ever met." Her soft brown eyes rested fondly on Jake. "You cooked for clients on our guided tours, you cleaned equipment, you helped with bus repairs, even through your, um—your family troubles. Sometimes I think Sam's Adventure Tours wouldn't be around if it weren't for you."

Jake flushed under her stare and lowered his eyes.

"I appreciate that you hired me, Nancy," he mumbled, trying to ignore that heavy feeling settling on him. He studied his plate and rubbed the back of his neck. It was true that Jake had worked his butt off. He'd needed a job. That was back when his dad had left the family. His mom had been so relieved when Jake had landed weekend work. And Nancy had known about his family problems and been kind to him. But he'd earned the job, he knew that. He still worked hard. That was just his way.

"Hey, I almost forgot to tell you, Nancy," Peter spoke up. "I just got my Red Cross lifeguard certificate. Worked for it all spring."

Nancy chuckled as she returned her attention to her clipboard. "That's good, Peter, though I hope we don't need you leaping into water as our clients board down mountain trails. So, Jake, your birthday's soon too, right? Sweet sixteen also?"

Peter laughed jeeringly and did a wolf whistle.

"Yeah, I'll be sixteen on July 31."

"Excellent," she said, noting it on her clipboard, then digging into her lunch.

They chatted lightly about the sport and upcoming trips, then amused themselves watching the kids splashing into the river, one by one. Black mountainboards, white kicker. White kicker, black river as a cloud moved in front of the sun. Nice that the river was deep, slow-moving, and free of obstacles where they'd set up the kicker, Jake thought. Jumping into water on a hot day really was a perfect way to get good at aerial tricks.

"Wait till I give you the signal to go!" a lifeguard stationed beside the kicker was shouting at the kids.

Jake scanned the lineup of boarders. "Hey, look at that tall guy with the shaved head. Maybe he's a parent? Nah, he looks too young."

"Sweet board," Peter observed. "And he's built like a wrestler. Maybe he knows what he's doing. Let's watch."

Nancy didn't comment; she was once again absorbed in writing on her clipboard.

Soon, the bald guy strapped his helmet on, climbed the steps to the kicker's roll-in, and set his board down on the lip. He stepped into his bindings and yanked them tight. He stretched his back by wrapping his hands around the opposite hip and pulling hard, looking back over his shoulder and down towards his front foot. A couple rolls of the neck and he hopped into the center of the roll-in. Then he launched forward and rocketed down the roll-in to the kicker. He powered off it to get so much air that Jake's neck cricked from watching him. Jake followed his form, enthralled, as the guy shot off the lip and into the air. Hardly had he left the ramp when the jumper turned his head, looking behind him. The rest of his body followed until it formed a giant twist. One, two, three full rotations, and he unwound himself just in time to set up his board to land incredibly smoothly into the water for a jump of that height. A 1080, executed perfectly.

Jake had only seen that trick attempted on videos a handful of times, and very seldom pulled off.

"Unbelievable," Peter muttered. "That guy rules!"

"A pro?" Jake wondered.

"Who're you talking about?" Nancy asked, lifting her head.

"The big, mean-looking dude swimming to the dock," Jake informed her.

Nancy laughed. "Mean? No, that's Jarrad. Wonder when he got here. You boys need to meet him."

She stood and waved at the guy, who waved back casually after lifting himself onto the dock like a gymnast. He removed his helmet and towel-dried his mountainboard off before himself. Then he hugged the board closely to his dark, muscle-ripped body. Jake watched him walk to a folding camp chair and lean down to exchange his helmet and life jacket for a hat and something else. He ambled toward them barefoot and shirtless, wearing only black boarding shorts, a black leather knife sheath, and the darkest tan Jake had ever seen. His chiseled face was now shadowed by a wide-rimmed, worn leather "bush" hat.

"G'day, boss," he greeted Nancy in a strong

Australian accent, tipping his hat. His clear blue eyes scanned Jake and Peter as he smiled at them. Jake noticed that even though he'd just emerged from the water, he had dirt under his fingernails.

"Good to see you," Nancy responded warmly. "Jarrad, meet Jake Evans and Peter Montpetit, the junior guides I've told you about. Jake and Peter, this is Jarrad Stopard, who's only just joined us at Sam's Adventure Tours. You'll be mountainboarding with him up on the forest trails this summer."

Jake shook the extended hand, which was firm and rough. A new guide who was an ace mountainboarder? Perfect! "Hi, Jarrad," Jake said enthusiastically. "Nice to meet you."

The man's grin widened, and he tipped the rim of his weathered hat again like a cowboy. "Heard all about you, Jake," he replied in a deep, gravelly voice.

"Hey, Jarrad," Peter said, stepping forward to pump the guy's hand. "Smooth trick, man. Awesome 1080! How long've you been boarding?"

Jarrad shook Peter's hand. "Hey, Peter. Heard all about you, too."

"Jarrad's been mountainboarding forever," Nancy informed the boys as she rested a hand on the younger man's knotted shoulder. "Anyway, Jarrad is a top-ranked racer in Australia," she continued, "even though he's only twenty-five. He also guided mountainboarding trips there. And he's great with kids, right Jarrad?"

"Love the little nippers," Jarrad confirmed, grinning freely at Nancy. Jake got the feeling that Jarrad felt pretty confident around the company manager, considering he was brand new and she was older and the most senior person in the company, not counting the owner Sam. He also got the feeling that Nancy thought Jarrad was okay. And Jake figured if Nancy liked him, then he had to be okay.

"So, we're nearly finished eating here—just watermelon left—but come join us anyway," Nancy invited Jarrad.

"That's choice. I'm starvin'," he said cheerfully, pulling his knife out of its waist sheath and playfully cutting the oversized watermelon slices in two, then lifting one to his mouth. "Be right with you. I'm off to fetch a beer first." He turned and left them with a friendly wave.

"So he's a new senior guide?" Jake asked Nancy.

"Yes," Nancy replied.

She was watching a red-shirted tyke maybe five years old fly off the kicker. He leaned forward like he was trying to grab the deck for a frontside grab. Jake winced even before he hit the water. Major belly flop, poor kid. The splashdown was ugly.

The lifeguard leaned forward to watch the water,

waiting for the boy to reappear. That's why he didn't see the next rider, a little girl waiting in the lineup, slip off the roll-in too soon, without the signal to go. Nancy must've sensed a disaster about to unfold. Jake and Peter sure did. But Peter turned out to have the fastest reaction. He leapt over the restaurant deck's railing, ran down the embankment, and dove into the water only seconds after the girl's board landed hard on the first kid's face.

Jake could hear splashing and screaming fill the air as he and Nancy ran down to the river's edge. The lineup of kids froze, waiting for the all-clear. The lifeguard tossed the life ring toward the confusion of splashing.

Peter emerged doing a lifeguard's tow of the little boy to shore. The boy's too-large helmet was askew and blood was flowing freely down his face. A hysterical woman was yelling and clutching her hair. Must be the boy's mom, Jake thought. She's totally freaking out. That's not going to help. He shook his head as the woman started jumping up and down close to the river's edge, pointing to her son.

The lifeguard waited until the little girl in the river had grabbed the life ring. Handing the rope end to a dad to pull in, he turned his attention to Peter and the boy. As he leaned down to help Peter lift the injured tyke to shore, Jake saw the dad accidentally drop the rope just as the little girl let go of the life ring while trying to grab her board as it floated by. Failing to reach the board or retrieve her hold on the ring, the little girl began to flail and scream in the water.

The girl was wearing a life jacket, but Jake decided she needed help. He took a big breath and dove in torpedo style. Wham! Something hit his shoulder and chest so hard he opened his mouth underwater trying to suck in the air that had just been knocked from him. His throat and nostrils burned as they took in water; his body felt bruised. Panic filled him as he fought to rise and breathe, only to come up against something blocking him from the surface.

He pushed against it, desperate for air. It was a body, kicking and flailing as much as he was. He pushed the weight away and surfaced. Gasping and coughing, he recognized the mother of the boy Peter had rescued, the one who'd been freaking out on the riverbank. She must have fallen in just as he'd dived.

She was still flailing like a madwoman. He looked from her to the sobbing girl to the life ring. Its rope was floating in front of his face. Chest still heaving, he reached for the rope just as the woman threw her arms around him in a panic, elbows digging into his back. Ouch! Her arms tightened around his neck, pushing him under before he could take another breath.

Once again, he was fighting for air. He could see

light filtering through a mass of bubbles and the woman's dark form immediately above him. He saw her knee move toward him even before his gut got the full brunt of it. Umph!

She didn't mean to, he told himself. She just can't swim and she's in full panic. Got … to … get … away from her so I can breathe. Then I can help her. He bowed his head and swept out his arms in an effort to swim downward so he could release her panicked hold. But her fingernails only pressed harder into his throat.

I'm stronger than she is, he told himself. Just … swim … down until she releases … that stranglehold.

But he was only pulling her beneath the surface, making her even more frightened. His lungs were now on fire, screaming for air, on the verge of exploding. He grabbed his assailant's forearms to lift them off his throat. Later he realized he should have stopped struggling to help her calm down, then moved behind her back where her panicked arms couldn't reach him. Then he could have towed her safely to shore the way Peter had the boy. He should have, but he was out of breath—so much so that panic engulfed him and the survival instinct kicked in. He lifted a fist and socked her one in the jaw, hard. Later, he'd have a hard time believing what he'd done.

She released him instantly as he surfaced and grabbed a breath, moving out of her reach. How was he to know his self-defense move had caused her to bite down hard on her tongue, drawing blood and a whole new volley of screams? Then, instead of moving to calm her, as he would have a second later having regained his sense, he simply grabbed the life ring's rope.

By then, Jarrad had sprinted down the hill and signaled the lifeguard not to jump in. Jarrad leapt into the river and brought the woman to shore, where he and Nancy turned her on her side. They bent over her as she made choking noises; then she vomited up river water mixed with blood.

"I can't swim! I can't swim!" the woman sobbed. "And he punched me—tried to drown me!" She pointed a shaking, dripping finger at Jake.

Nancy and the new guide looked quizzically at Jake.

Numbly, Jake grabbed the little girl by her life jacket and finished towing her, her board, and the life ring to shore.

"Grandpa!" she cried as she ran into the arms of a concerned-looking man.

Meanwhile, the soaked, sniffling woman wrapped her arms around the boy Peter had rescued. The tyke was grinning sheepishly, tissues stuck up his nostrils, patches of drying blood beneath them.

"Just a bloody nose, luckily," Peter was saying.

"Nice save," Nancy called over to Peter before

retrieving her clipboard and turning her gaze briefly on Jake. Her eyes held the same dark disappointment he'd seen when he flunked his first-aid course. Worse, Jarrad's intense blue eyes seemed to be sizing him up.

3 Road Trip

"Minibus or big bus?" Peter asked. He set his backpack down on the garage floor but kept his mountainboard tucked under his arm. He was really excited about this first Sam's Adventure Tours mountainboarding trip, especially with it being just a few hours' drive from where he lived. Peter lived in Seattle, a short bike ride from where Sam ran his American operations out of an office and a garage filled with sports equipment.

"Minibus," Nancy replied as she and Jarrad entered the garage hefting a heavy container of camping gear between them. "No clients this trip, remember? Just guides."

Perfect, Peter thought. Good chance to make sure he impressed both Nancy and Jarrad. And a great opportunity to get lots of pointers from Jarrad. That's surely why Sam had hired Jarrad, he figured, to help fine-tune Jake's and Peter's mountainboarding skills. Just last week, Peter had overheard Sam saying to Nancy, "Jake and Peter are coming along, but they haven't totally mastered it yet, don't you agree?"

Nancy had stuck up for them, insisting they were improving quickly. Then Sam had said, "And you know I want twice as many girls signing up for our trips as last year, right? There's a whole untapped market there, I think."

He'd seen Nancy nod, then hang her head, which had seemed kind of strange.

"No clients this trip, just us," Jake was echoing Nancy's reminder. "So we get to know the trails before we take a pack of kids down them, right?" He plopped down on his backpack and started playing with a new compass he'd bought. As they waited for Nancy to unlock the van, Peter looked at Jake's compass with envy.

"Exactly," Nancy said, although Peter thought for a second that she seemed to be avoiding his eyes. She unlocked the van's rear door. "Okay, everyone pitch in with loading up."

"Hey, this thing's way heavy," Jarrad exclaimed as he lifted Peter's pack. "What have you got in it, Peter, barbells?"

"Books," Peter said, feeling proud.

Jarrad snorted and shook his head. "Leave 'em

home, dude. They've got no place on a guide training trip."

"Sure they do," Peter spoke up confidently. "I've got some on orienteering and wilderness survival. Even one about volcanoes." The kind of stuff that outdoor guides should know, he thought. Things Jarrad probably already knew from guiding in Australia.

Jarrad paused and shot Peter a dark look, then seemed to reconsider. He shrugged, smiled, and placed a teasing hand on Peter's head. "Well, they might come in handy as fire starter, anyway."

Very funny, Peter thought, confident that despite the joke, Jarrad had been impressed. Right before this trip, his mom had given him a big lecture about doing "summer reading." Then she'd taken him to a bookstore and let him buy any ten books he wanted. Any ten! She wasn't too pleased when he bought only wilderness survival books, but too bad. He was pretty stoked about his stash of reading, whether it meant a heavy backpack or not.

"Let him take as many books as he wants," Jake spoke up, hoisting his own pack into the van. "Shuts him up for a while."

Nancy and Jarrad chuckled, the boys made faces at each other, and soon everything was in and Nancy was backing the vehicle out of the garage.

"So, three days on Mount Hood, then three on

Mount Adams, then three on Mount St. Helens," Nancy reminded them. "Want to be my map reader, Jake?"

"Yeah," Jake replied.

Peter tried not to feel passed over. Jake had worked for Sam's Adventure Tours longer than he had. So Nancy knew Jake better, and maybe couldn't help treating him like her favorite. But it kind of steamed Peter sometimes that she didn't even try to hide it. Being a teacher's pet was kind of sucky.

Peter had passed his first-aid course with a top score, first try. Jake had flunked and needed to retake it. And Peter had done that river rescue even before the lifeguard knew what was going on, while poor old Jake had leapt in a bit late and blown it after that. But had that made any difference with Nancy? No.

Okay, stop being a whiner, Peter told himself. It was small-minded to be jealous of his best friend when Jake had gotten him this job in the first place.

But Peter had an agenda on this trip that no one knew about. A secret he wasn't about to spill even to Jake. And the only way things could turn out the way he wanted was to get Nancy—and now Jarrad too—to notice him more. That, and doing everything right this trip. He needed to be the best junior guide Sam's Adventure Tours had ever had. His new collection of survival books was just a small part of succeeding in his secret quest.

"I've been on Mount Hood tons of times," Peter spoke up. "My family goes camping there almost every summer." Okay, so he was exaggerating a little, but Nancy and Jake were from Canada and Jarrad was Australian, so Peter needed to remind them that this trip was in his backyard, so to speak.

"That's good, Peter. Know anything about its northwest flank?" Nancy asked.

"Um, I'd have to look at a map, but probably," Peter replied.

"Nancy and I spent a couple of weeks this spring checking it out," Jarrad spoke up in his deep, rumbly voice while fingering a rabbit's foot key ring. "We found some good trails, and Nancy worked hard to get us permits to run trips on them."

Peter felt as deflated as a popped balloon. Nancy hadn't even mentioned Jarrad before she'd introduced him to the boys, and now it turns out that she and Jarrad had spent weeks together choosing the trails already? As if Jake and Peter couldn't have offered some advice?

Okay, Peter scolded himself, get a grip. Nancy's the boss woman, and you and Jake are just itsy-bitsy junior guides, lucky to have this job. And Jarrad is Mister Mountainboarder, so he's way more qualified to choose trails even if he only just blew in from Oz. Peter peered at Jarrad, sitting tall in the van's front seat. His leather hat with the floppy brim made him look like some Wild West cowboy; the rabbit's foot on the key ring he'd set down on the dashboard looked real. He was paring an apple with his giant knife, the one he usually kept sheathed on his belt.

"So Jarrad," Peter said, "how long have you been in the Northwest and how come you came here?"

"A year, mate," he replied. "No reason. Just thought I'd give it a bash."

"And mountainboarding is a big thing Down Under?" Peter would show him he could talk like an "Aussie" too.

"It's a free sport for the free world," Jarrad replied, turning his head to smile at Nancy. "Surfers like mountainboarding when the waves aren't up. Mountainboarding is dirt surfing. And Australia's got lots of dirt." He chuckled and Nancy smiled.

"So tell us some crazy things you've done on your board," Peter urged.

"Yeah, what're your best tricks?" Jake joined in.

Jarrad finished paring the apple, wiped his knife shiny clean on his T-shirt, and stowed it back in its leather sheath. He crunched into the apple as if needing a moment to mentally flip through his thick "crazy-rides" file.

"My parents own a cattle station," he began. "That means we've got a couple of strong working dogs.

Strong enough to tow us into some big dirt jumps when I hook 'em up to a tow rope."

"That sounds fun, but it isn't crazy," Peter observed. "A friend of mine gets his brother to tow him like that with his quad. And I know someone else whose dad does it with his golf cart."

"I once got a speeding ticket while boarding," Jarrad allowed.

"You mean coming down a road?" Jake asked.

"No, in a park. This parks officer sees me and reckons I'm doin' fifty miles per hour. He waits till I get to the bottom and says I can't do that sort of sport in the park. I tell him to rack off. And he tickets me."

"Come on," Peter said. "You've done crazier stuff than that, I bet." He liked Jarrad's accent and expressions.

"Maybe he doesn't want you getting into trouble by copying whatever stunts he's done," Nancy suggested teasingly, slowing the van a little at the mention of a speeding ticket.

"Okay, once a coupla mates and I rode down a ten-storey car park. You know, where the exit ramp goes down and around a big pillar? On the seventh level, we set up a rail to grind on. So, we were taking some tight turns and that concrete was real hard. By the time we reached the third level, we were taking some nasty spills. Took us a few tries to get it wired. Big-time road rash. Will that do?"

"Tell me one more," Peter dared him.

Jarrad did a dramatic sigh, finished off his apple, and turned to survey Jake and Peter with that deeply tanned face and blue eyes. He offered them a conspiratorial grin and lowered his voice to a stage whisper.

"You mean besides leaping off roofs, riding nude in the middle of the night, and bashing into the mother of all kangaroos—man, that's like hitting a brick wall!"

Peter and Jake both smiled and nodded their heads.

"Right-o. Not too far west of Sydney are the Blue Mountains, a pretty wild mountain range."

"Uh-huh," the boys said.

"We found this concrete pipe there that was part of the Snowy River system. It was twenty feet wide and ran about a mile. That's something like twelve city blocks long, and it was totally pitch-dark inside."

Peter liked the sound of this story.

"It went underground all that way. And in summer it was dry as week-old wombat dung."

"What's a wombat?" Jake asked quizzically.

"Looks like a big teddy bear crossed with a dog. Lives in burrows like a giant chipmunk, and carries its babies in a pouch like a kangaroo. It's Australian, mate."

"Oh."

"So we headed down this pipe on our boards. Figured it'd be an easy ride, that we'd get to work up some speed, maybe hit thirty miles an hour. Didn't reckon on some idiot who didn't know we were there opening the sluice gate and letting water out when we were about halfway down and still underground."

Peter noticed Nancy listening as closely as the boys.

"We heard this rumbling behind us. And we could feel the cool air it was pushing in front of it. We heard it coming as it was splashing off the walls. And we knew we had to either outrun it or get a rough spin."

Peter didn't need that last expression translated. "And?" he demanded.

"We tucked up real aerodynamic-like to gain speed and rode out of the pipe and into daylight just ahead of a wave of water. I slid into some nasty blackberry bushes. Then we had to get out of there before we got caught for trespassing. Talk about a rush."

"Is that story for real?" Jake asked, eyes lit up.

"It's fair dinkum," the Aussie confirmed.

"Don't try that trick at home," said Nancy.

Everyone laughed. They chatted for miles. They watched trees blink by. They learned Aussie songs, with Jarrad shouting "bleep" anytime there were rude words in the lyrics, which was a lot. Shortly before they hit the Washington/Oregon border, both the boys and Jarrad voted for a break to stretch their legs. Nancy pulled off the freeway and parked the minibus next to a big tour bus at a rest stop beside a clear blue lake.

"Yes, yes, yes!" Peter said, eyebrows going up as he

surveyed the big bus and the lake. "Look what we've got!" The tour bus beside them was emptying itself of girls. Girls who were Jake's and Peter's age. As if an entire girls' school was on a school trip. Some of the girls were heading from the bus to a changing shed beside the lake. Others were emerging from the changing room in swimming suits, laughing and chatting as they spread their towels out on the sand.

"Good timing, Nance," Peter added, doing a low whistle. "They're all lookers." He dug in his pack for his Frisbee, swimsuit, and towel.

"I get the redhead in the yellow bikini," Jake joked, rooting through his own pack for his swim gear.

"Okay, and I get the blonde in the red sparkly suit. Is she built or what?"

"Boys," Nancy teased with a smile. "We're just taking a twenty-minute break here. No harassing anyone."

"Sheilas," Jarrad intoned in a disgusted voice. "Trouble, all of 'em. Steer clear if you have any sense, boys."

Peter laughed as he donned his shades, leapt out of the van, and sprinted for the changing room, Jake not far behind. He remembered that Australians sometimes called girls "Sheilas" and boys "Bruces."

"Good thing we've picked different girls," Peter kidded Jake as he whipped off his T-shirt. On one trip, he and Jake had fallen for the same client, a good-looking French girl who'd flirtatiously played them off each other. Bad idea, bad scene. So the friends had sworn they'd never do that again. They'd agreed to check with each other when some girl interested them. Of course, Nancy had warned them not to go for clients.

"Good thing," Jake teased back as he grabbed the Frisbee and headed out of the changing room toward the largest gathering of giggling girls. "Not that we have the same taste, anyway."

"You've got that right. And hey, that's my Frisbee," Peter called out, running to catch up.

4 New Girl

"Seems like you packed an awful lot of food and gear for us," Jake observed as they unloaded the van at their campsite a few hours later. "There's just the four of us, right?"

He watched Nancy set her clipboard down on a picnic table and exchange smiles with Jarrad. "Actually," Nancy said, "there are two others joining us."

"Your boyfriend is one of them?" Peter guessed as he dropped his and Jake's tent bag on some flat ground.

"All right!" Jake said. "Haven't seen Angus in ages!" He and Peter both liked Nancy's boyfriend a lot. They'd been on many trips together.

"Nope," Nancy said, smiling.

"Some other senior guides, then," Peter guessed. Jake and Peter were the only junior guides in the company.

"Nope."

"But you said there weren't any clients on this trip, that we were just learning the trails before we did a client trip," Jake reminded her.

"True." She was smiling mysteriously, or maybe even evasively. Jake didn't like her keeping secrets. Secrets like Jarrad. Jarrad was fun, and Jake liked the idea of an expert mountainboarder being on staff. Still, it wasn't like Nancy to spring things on them.

"Girls?" Peter asked hopefully.

Jake had to smile. Peter was way into girls these days. Not that Jake had any objection to girls. He was shyer around them, tended to freeze up or talk nonsense when one paid attention to him, but he was always on the lookout for an interesting girl. Peter was the smooth talker, the confident one, the one girls usually fell for easily. And Peter always went for the vivacious, fun-loving, drop-dead gorgeous ones. Jake preferred quiet types and always took his time before deciding if he really liked someone. Looks weren't as important to him, even if he pretended otherwise around Peter.

"Yes, girls," Nancy revealed, tapping her clipboard as Jarrad set up the cooking area. "The one you'll meet first is Susanna. She has applied to be a junior guide. She's fifteen and her references say she's a very skilled mountainboarder with some guiding experience. Also, her dad is a good friend of Sam's." Jake wondered if he was imagining a shadow flick briefly across Nancy's face as she said that. "She'll be joining us shortly. Her sister is a former top-ranked dirt boardercross racer and has also done some guiding. I'm sure you two will cooperate in showing them the ropes." Nancy paused and her eyebrows drew together. "And treating them as young gentlemen would."

"Gentlemen?!" Jarrad jeered loudly from in front of his tent. "These two?" He belly-laughed and shook his head. "Sheilas. Always a pack of trouble."

"And that goes for you too," Nancy said, turning to Jarrad and standing tall with the clipboard against her chest. Her voice was both teasing and stern, just enough to make Jarrad lift his thumb to signal that he'd got the message.

"We'll be true, gentlemanly representatives of Sam's Adventure Tours," Peter reported with a salute.

Saluting Nancy was cheeky, Jake thought. Peter should be more respectful. "No worries," Jake said to her.

Jarrad was new. This Susanna was new. And Nancy hadn't mentioned either one of them to the boys till just before she'd felt like introducing them. Jake was glad the company was growing. He was just a little unsettled about the suddenness of it all. But a girl junior guide. Or junior guide applicant, he corrected himself. That was a change.

Jake hoped this Susanna and her sister would be gutsy and hard-working. And preferably not too good-looking or it would be distracting. And that Jarrad, who seemed to have a thing against girls unless he was just joking, would be decent to them. Good practice for Jarrad if the company was pushing to get more girl customers, anyway.

"So, Sam's really expanding his business lately," Jake observed.

"Yes, just trying some new people," Nancy confirmed, nodding as she looked toward Jarrad, who was trimming some hot dog roasting sticks. "Let's get camp set up before they come."

The four of them managed to set up all their tents, organize and stow the gear, and help prepare supper before they heard a car with a noisy muffler approaching.

The growl of a handbrake accompanied the sound of the car coughing to a stop.

"Nancy Sheppard?" the driver asked. He was a light-haired, middle-aged man in jeans and a fleece jacket. "You must be Nancy, Sam Miller's manager? Sam speaks highly of you. He and I go way back, you know."

"Yes, I'm Nancy," she replied, stepping forward. "John Michaelson? Sam says you two grew up together. Pleased to meet you. And this must be Susanna."

She moved to offer her hand to the slim blonde emerging with a wide smile from the passenger side. "Welcome, Susanna. We've been looking forward to meeting you."

"Same," said the girl, pumping Nancy's arm.

Jake looked her over quickly. Her long, wavy blonde hair was drawn back loosely with a sparkly barrette. A silver locket hung around her tanned neck. Her short jean skirt revealed long, shapely legs. Her outdoor sandals were sturdy yet fashionable. Her face … well, she had the radiant looks of a teen model who'd just stepped off the runway. She was hands-down the most stunning girl Jake had ever seen.

He looked over at Peter. Someone, he thought darkly, needs to push Peter's unhinged jaw up and poke his popped-out eyes back into their sockets. Jake turned to see Jarrad flick his eyes over the new girl once, frown, and then bend back over his work, his hat brim shadowing whatever expression was on his face.

Australian men, Jake mused, had a reputation for being a bit hard on females. But Nancy would make him treat Susanna okay.

"Susanna," Nancy was saying, ignoring the fact that Peter had appeared at her elbow and was all but panting to be introduced, "this is Jake Evans, who has been with our outfit longer than almost anyone. And he does so many sports that I can't even name them off any more." She smiled and placed a gentle hand on Jake's back to push him forward for a handshake with Susanna.

"Hi, Susanna," Jake said, trying his best to lift his eyes to her long-lashed, sparkling blue ones. "Welcome to Sam's Adventure Tours."

She shook his hand firmly, her face glowing with excitement. "Nice to meet you, Jake. Nancy says you're the best! I've been so stoked to meet you."

Jake felt himself blushing big time. He released her warm hand and backed away a step, studying the ground. He could think of no words to respond to that. He just stood there stupidly, rubbing the back of his neck.

"Hi, Susanna. I'm Peter Montpetit," Peter spoke up, not waiting for Nancy to introduce him. "About time Nancy hired another junior guide. Welcome aboard. Anything you need to know, just ask me."

Jake looked up long enough to see that Peter was holding more than shaking her hand and giving her that look that he always gave girls he called "hot." A look that said he knew he was a chick magnet and that she'd be unable to resist him.

Give her a break, Jake wanted to say.

"Peter's also a junior guide," Nancy informed Susanna, resting a hand on Susanna's arm and pulling her away. "So, come meet Jarrad, Australia's mountainboarding legend."

"G'day, Susanna!" boomed Jarrad's voice.

Jake turned to the all-but-forgotten dad behind them. "Hi, Mr. Michaelson," he addressed the man, who was unloading a mountainboard and a lumpy canvas gear bag from his car's trunk. "Are you joining us for supper?"

"Thanks, but no, I'll push off right away," he said. "Need to get back to Portland to pick up my other daughter from a mountainboard race and take her to another. Little local races, nothing big like she used to do. Nice to meet you, though. Bye, Susanna!" he called out to his daughter.

"Oh, bye Dad!" she said cheerily, sprinting over and giving him a quick hug, then returning to talk with Nancy.

Mr. Michaelson looked from Jake to Peter. "I'd say look after Susanna, but she's very good at looking after herself and everyone else," he said proudly. "She's our liveliest one, that's for sure. A real chatterbox. And loves tearing down trails on this thing," he added, placing her well-used mountainboard on top of the bag he'd set down. "So have fun and see you in a week. Give my regards to Sam."

"You bet!" Peter enthused as Susanna's father waved at Nancy, Jarrad, and his daughter, then climbed back into his car. The muffler belched as he turned the Ford around and headed down the mountain. Oregon license plate, Jake noticed.

"Grub's on," Jarrad called.

Jake and Peter needed no further invitation to move toward the crackling campfire and accept sticks with hot dogs pushed onto them.

"First dibs," Peter whispered fervently before Susanna joined them. Jake presumed he wasn't talking about hot dog sticks. The five campers soon settled in a circle around the fire, their sticks over the flames as the hot dogs sizzled and browned.

"I'm so excited," Susanna was saying. "Can't believe I get to mountainboard Mount Hood. It's a sleeping volcano, right? With real gnarly trails?" she asked no one in particular. She carried on so quickly that no one had time to answer her. "It's steeper around here than where I live. We live near Crater Lake, like four hours south of here. It's a big lake in a crater that a volcano left when it blew up like two hundred years ago. There's a whole club of boarders there, and we ..."

Chatterbox was a good word for her, Jake mused as Susanna rattled on and on, mostly about boarding. Her body was in constant motion as she talked. She certainly wasn't shy. Hyperactive might be a better description. Nancy seemed pleased to hear about Susanna's life and activities. Peter's eyes were so glued to her that he burned two hot dogs in a row. Jarrad retreated to wander in the woods nearby.

"I'm finished eating and it's still light out," Susanna declared a while later. "Can we go boarding now?"

"As soon as the dishes are washed," Nancy replied.

"You bet. I'll do them," Susanna offered.

"I'll help," Peter spoke up quickly.

Hmmm, Jake thought. Score one for the new girl if she's going to be a good influence on Peter's work habits.

Half an hour later, the three youths left Nancy and Jarrad talking business at camp and scouted out a nearby clearing with natural hillocks to use as a play park. As Jake cleared some sticks and rocks from potential runs, Peter and Susanna warmed up. Soon all three were carrying their boards up and running them down the small rises, pulling easy maneuvers, laughing, and chatting. Peter was hanging on Susanna's every word and upping the ante on every trick like the showoff he was. Susanna, Jake noticed, had an easy, relaxed style. She'd clearly been at the sport a while.

"Hey!" Peter said after they'd been boarding for half an hour. "Wanna try racing?"

"Sure," came two replies.

But on his very first run, Peter crashed big trying to go too fast. "Ouch!" he said, looking embarrassed the second he'd said it.

"Peter! Are you okay?" Susanna asked, rushing over and kneeling beside him as he held his knee and tried not to grimace.

"He's fine," Jake said with a touch of sarcasm, annoyed that Peter had claimed Susanna so quickly, without even trying to discuss it with Jake first. "Like Nancy says, he just has an overactive set of lungs."

Susanna looked at Jake questioningly.

"The level of pain someone seems to have does not always indicate the danger they are in," Jake advised her, quoting Nancy.

5 Two and One

Early the next morning, Nancy drove them high up the mountain in a mist that clung lightly to the minibus and surrounding trees, following a logging road that could hardly be called a road. Peter felt his body bounced and jarred as the trusty little vehicle jounced steadily upwards over dried-mud ruts the size of street curbs. Peter eyed the map in his lap and shook his head.

"Crazy ride, hey?" He grinned at Susanna, whom he'd maneuvered to sit beside in the back seat this morning. "Only Nancy would take this on."

"Totally," Susanna agreed with a dazzling smile that threatened to melt him. "Can't wait to board this mountain." She popped a hard candy into her mouth.

She was wearing body-hugging boarding trousers and a long-sleeved khaki shirt unbuttoned just far enough to reveal a red shirt beneath it with a low, scooped neck. Her heart-shaped silver locket bounced above that neckline along with the van, which was surely testing its shocks on this trip. Peter's eyes were on the locket, and he was hoping there wasn't a boyfriend's photo in there. Just then the van broke through the mist and sunshine glinted off the locket's silver. He raised his head as Nancy slowed to a stop.

"Best viewpoint on Mount Hood," Nancy announced, grabbing her camera from the glove compartment as everyone piled out. "And good light this time of morning."

It wasn't even nine o'clock yet. Peter, standing so close to Susanna that he could smell the peppermint candy in her mouth, swept his eyes slowly around the stunning panorama. He took off his baseball cap to feel the sun's warming rays on his head. Below them, light clouds swirled to hide everything but the tops of three mountains, including the one on which they were standing. Just above them, snow dazzled his eyes. It was like arriving in heaven and finding three black islands floating in a sea of white. Three black islands like scoops of licorice ice cream sprayed with whipped cream, because each revealed a cap of snow on its top, even now in midsummer.

He breathed in the fresh mountain air accented with Susanna's peppermint and shook his head in awe.

"Mount Hood, Mount Adams, and Mount St.

Helens," he said. "The Native Americans around here have a legend about these three volcanoes. The legend says Mount Hood and Mount Adams were brothers who both fell in love with Mount St. Helens, who was a shapely maiden. Two boys, one girl. Formula for trouble, hey?" he joked.

"Mount St. Helens was a beautiful, shapely mountain before it erupted in 1980," Nancy inserted. "I've seen photos of it. And it's almost finished recovering enough that you could call it shapely again. I think I've heard this legend, but go on."

"Hood and Adams got so violent in their fight over her that they started shaking and belching smoke and fire. The sky went dark and thundery, rivers turned brown, animals ran away. St. Helens tried to stop the two brothers from fighting, but she couldn't. Finally, all three collapsed, so exhausted that they went to sleep. And the Great Spirit came and rewarded St. Helens for trying to stop the fight by making her a beautiful, shapely maiden again."

"Two males, one female. Sounds like they needed another lady mountain," Jake commented dryly.

"And your point is?" Jarrad asked Peter, removing his hat and swatting at mosquitoes with it.

"That's how the first people around here explained how all three erupted basically at the same time, and how St. Helens recovered the best and the fastest — her forests and rivers, and the animals that came back or whatever. That's exactly what has happened several times in the past two thousand years."

"That's so epic," Susanna said, stretching her long arms high to the sky. "How'd you know that?"

"From some books I brought with me," Peter replied, leaning suavely against the van and wriggling his eyebrows at her. "I'll show them to you later."

He could flirt with her if he wanted to. Not because he'd called first dibs on her against Jake, but because Jake had admitted last night that she was way too excitable and talkative to be his type. Good thing because she was totally Peter's type and he could hardly believe his luck that Sam was looking to hire someone like her. A mountainboard chick who looked like a movie star. Perfect.

"And when are they scheduled to erupt again?" Susanna asked, shifting her feet as she stared from one mountaintop to another.

"That's the million-dollar question," Peter asserted. "Any one of 'em could go anytime again. Scientists can't say exactly when."

"Well then, Scientist Montpetit, we'd better get boarding, don't you think?" Jarrad asked with dripping sarcasm, climbing back into the van.

Half an hour later, as the clouds cleared away, Nancy pulled over to a trail. "Unloading time," she announced. “This is the start of the trail. It finishes where we’re camped. Jarrad figures two hours to the bottom. I’ll be there in camp waiting for you when you arrive.”

“Okay, you two dirty dogs and Sheila,” Jarrad kidded them, “kit yourselves up.”

“He means get our helmets and body armor on,” Peter interpreted for Susanna as Jarrad moved out of earshot.

“Like I can’t figure that out,” she giggled. “He’s great, isn’t he? A Crocodile Dundee like in the movies. ‘G’day mates,’” she tried to mimic him.

“A character and an amazing boarder,” Jake reminded them. “Guess we’ll really see his stuff today.”

Peter was still pulling on his elbow pads when he saw Jake wandering around in circles with his compass in his hand, watching the needle.

“This way’s northeast,” Jake announced, pointing a finger.

“We can tell that from the fact that Mount Adams is sitting there,” Susanna responded, pointing and smiling. She was never not smiling, Peter reflected happily.

“And that way”—Peter pointed to Mount St. Helens—“is northwest. Then, straight north a hundred miles is Mount Rainier, beside Seattle. The four volcanoes form a sort of diamond shape, with the Washington/Oregon border running across the middle.”

Jake looked up sheepishly. "Well, if the mountains weren't showing, my compass would tell us the direction."

Duh, Peter thought. Poor old Jake is so fixated on his new compass, he forgets to look up sometimes.

"Okay, mates," Jarrad said, pocketing his rabbit-foot keychain. "Everyone ready to go?"

"Yeah!" Susanna answered, stepping into her bindings and tightening them over her shoes.

"I'll wait for a minute in case someone decides they've forgotten something essential," Nancy said, climbing into the minibus and sticking her head out of the rolled-down window. Nancy did lots of sports, Peter reflected, but she hadn't taken up mountainboarding. She was thirty, kind of old to take up something new. Mountainboarding was pretty hard on the bod, even with a helmet, long-sleeved clothing, padded-seat shorts, and armor on your wrists, knees, and elbows.

"Okay," Jarrad said, standing on his bright red board and looking impressive in his black helmet and armor. "Now yesterday, I noticed you were putting too much pop in your pump, Peter. That's why you nosedive sometimes. And Jake, really think about your windup before you start a spin, so you have enough to complete a trick. Susanna, when you lean forward for speed, keep your weight balanced better. You're all good mountainboarders, but this is the chance to get better before we have clients to guide down. And Susanna, if we get girl clients, you pay special attention to making sure they're happy. They'll be looking up to you 'cause you're a girl. Sam says that's important."

Peter thought that last comment sounded a little forced, like Sam or Nancy had drilled it into Jarrad and he felt he had to say it.

"You tell them," Nancy called to Jarrad as she started up the minibus and waved goodbye. The Aussie lifted his head, smiled, and waved at her. Then he pointed down the dirt trail and they all fell into line.

"So, like I was saying," Jarrad said in a booming voice, "you three galas—that means idiots—better pull it together before the boss brings on brats for you to babysit."

Peter laughed. "Dare you to say that when Sam or Nancy is in earshot."

"Not a chance," Jarrad said, winking at Peter.

The first hour, they spoke little, just concentrated hard on the steep terrain. Jarrad didn't coach them much but issued pointers now and again. The second hour, as the vertical got less intense, Jarrad challenged them with exercises like leaping over a log and rolling the body correctly when falling.

"I ripped my knee apart once when I was doing a

power slide and got spat into a log that was hiding in some tall grass," Jarrad told them. "You have to scout a route first. Gotta train your impulses to do the moves that get you 'round objects jumpin' out and surprisin' you."

"Oh well, so much for this jacket," Susanna laughed after a practice roll caked hers with mud, thorns, and a little blood from an arm scratch.

Peter was impressed. Mountainboarding didn't attract many girls because of the danger and grime factor. But maybe Sam's latest push would help change that. Anyway, some girls were sporty, like Susanna. And you couldn't learn without falling. Take Jarrad, for example. The guy's chest, back, arms, and legs looked like a Grand Central Station of railroad-shaped scars. Probably meant he hadn't always worn full body armor. One way or another, he looked like he'd earned his skills the hard way. And now he was passing his wisdom on to the junior guides and junior guide trainee, joking around and whistling on his way down Mount Hood. It was hard not to like him, even if he was a little rough around the edges. Peter wondered if Jarrad had any books on mountainboarding he could borrow.

The third hour, when Susanna punctured a tire, Jarrad burst into an out-of-tune rendition of "Oh! Susanna," as he produced a wrench and a spare hub from his backpack. He watched approvingly as she fixed it by herself. "You should try the new aluminum hubs," he suggested, then went into a long-winded explanation of the best and newest equipment for the sport, continuing it even as they wound down the path.

Peter wished he knew half as much as Jarrad and was even half as skilled on his board. At least Jarrad was too old to elbow in on Susanna, he thought ruefully, not that Jarrad seemed to like girls anyway.

Peter made sure he was riding just ahead of Susanna and turning around lots to smile at her, even if it cost him a few bruising body barrel rolls. He noticed that Jake had to bail on a steep section or two, as well. Even Susanna, whose board slides were really powerful when she was going for it, fell several times. Then there was Jarrad. The only time he hit the dirt all morning, Peter noticed, was when he was demonstrating how to fall.

Jarrad got them singing crazy Aussie songs as they cruised like a chain of champions toward camp. The breeze they created by flowing down the trail was a perfect antidote to the ever-hotter sun. Nice, too, that even while hurtling downhill at thirty miles per hour, Peter thought he could hear birds singing along with them from the trees. This is a perfect day, he thought exuberantly. Mountainboarding all the way down a forest trail with a cool senior guide, a cute girl, and my best friend—on a warm summer morning with lunch waiting and no little kids to guide. And this guides-only trip has two more mountains to go: two "brothers" and a "fair maiden" sleeping peacefully and picturesquely less than sixty miles from one another.

6 Descent

Jake was taking a ton of tumbles that morning, but he didn't mind. He knew he wasn't as good a boarder as he probably should be to guide mountainboarding trips, but he was pretty close. Even Sam had said so just before this trip, though he'd said it in a grumpy kind of way: "Pretty close, boys." All Jake needed was a little coaching from Jarrad, he figured. By the end of the week, he'd be there. Impossible to be equally good at all the sports Sam's Adventure Tours did, after all.

It was a warm, clear day, the trail had all the features a mountainboarder could wish for, and the scenery was breathtaking. Between the occasional spills, he was boarding his best ever, if he could say so himself.

He liked that all his companions were skilled, enthusiastic, and fun. He didn't mind Peter showing off for Susanna; that was totally predictable. It was nice having a girl in their group, and Jake got a kick out of her high-energy personality the same way he liked Peter's effervescent self. As long as Jake could retreat from them now and again, or tease them into calming down, no problem. The girl was not only a good boarder, but a looker. And she looked incredible in anything she wore. If she were a quieter, more reflective girl, Jake would've had difficulty giving Peter first dibs. But ninety percent of the time, he was okay with just admiring Susanna's looks from afar and letting Peter try to win her.

More than two-thirds of the way down the hill, Peter pointed to some dirt mounds, bigger and more challenging than the ones they'd played on their first evening on Hood.

"Hey, Jarrad! Check it out! Okay to stop here and try some freestyle?" he asked.

"Why not?" Jarrad replied.

Jake paused and turned around to check on Susanna, only to see her front binding snap as she tried to slide left through a turn just before the mounds.

"No way!" she cried in frustration as she picked up her board. "One of my bindings has worked loose. Looks like the nuts dropped off on the trail somewhere," she muttered, frowning.

"Lousy, but we're gettin' close to camp now," Jarrad

said. "You could try ridin' fakie and takin' it real slow so at least your front foot's strapped down. Then we'll fix it at camp."

Susanna nodded. "Yeah, guess that's what I'll have to do."

"Give us ten minutes here first?" Peter asked her.

She smiled at him. "You guys go ahead without me. I'll head down. Maybe I'll even have it fixed by the time you get there."

"If you want," Jarrad said, nodding slowly. "Just keep on the trail and you can't get lost. There's nuts in my tool box in the minibus."

"Perfect," she said. "See you later." With one foot strapped down, she wove down the trail slo-mo, humming.

Jarrad shook his head with a faint smile as he looked at Peter and Jake. "It'll sure be quiet the rest of the way to camp."

Not unless Peter disappears too, Jake thought playfully.

Jake didn't mind pulling tricks off this dirt jump for a little while. "Sweet!" he shouted when Peter managed a Stalefish Air—grabbing the board with his back hand beside his inside back foot, then laying his body parallel to the ground, releasing his hand, and landing forward.

But after Jake jumped over the back of a smaller

berm and landed in prickly bushes, he retired under a tree and pulled out his compass, trying to guess north and south without looking at it. When that lost his interest, he stood up stiffly and said, "I'm out of here, okay? See you at camp."

"See you there," the other two said distractedly as Jarrad caught enough air to demonstrate a 540: rotating one and a half times, then landing switch-stance.

Fifteen minutes later, Jake spotted wild blueberry bushes just as camp came into view. He stopped, lifted off his helmet, and slipped his feet out of his bindings to gather some into his helmet. He was so busy berry-picking he almost didn't notice Susanna sitting quietly at the picnic table across the clearing. A sunbeam had chosen to shine on her as the rest of camp lay shadowed by tall cedars. It made her blonde hair golden and caused her silver locket to wink at Jake. One side of her face was shrouded in shadow, and she was holding a book and reading, still wearing her mountainboarding gloves. She'd changed into white jeans and a long-sleeved black T-shirt, a strange choice for a hot day, Jake thought. She had on serious skater shoes, complete with a thick, padded tongue. They looked brand-new, a spotless white. He hadn't seen her in them before. She must have washed her hair too, for instead of being curly and in a clasp, it formed a ponytail that flopped over her right shoulder.

Something was different about her, Jake thought as he placed his helmet of berries in the crook of his arm and continued gazing at her. She was quiet and studious, that's what. Not tapping a finger or foot, or squirming about like usual, or talking at Nancy, who wasn't in sight. He sighed. If Peter weren't on this trip and she was quiet and meditative like this more often, Jake would fall for her. Even now, he could feel something stirring in his chest, something he needed to suppress. She was beautiful, that's all. Stunningly beautiful. It didn't mean he had to like her in that way. He'd already told Peter he wasn't interested.

Susanna must have sensed someone staring at her because she put the book down and looked about. Jake strode into camp carrying his board and berries, about to greet her. She turned toward him, and he halted in his tracks. She'd left the group only half an hour earlier, but what kind of disaster had she met on the way down the trail? One side of her face wore a scar that made him wince. That's when Nancy entered the clearing carrying a bucket of water.

"Jake," she said, as Jake tried to pull his eyes away from the dark side of Susanna's pale face. "You're back. Susanna and I were just fetching some water from the stream. And you haven't met Melissa yet. Melissa is Susanna's identical twin sister."

The real Susanna appeared behind Nancy with her

usual gregarious smile, swinging her bucket so much that water was splashing out its sides.

"Hey, Jake," she said, setting the bucket down and walking over to place an arm around her double. Double except for the scar, Jake thought. "Meet my sister, Melissa. You'll like her. We look alike, but she's not as hyper as me, right Mel?"

Melissa smiled. It was almost a Susanna smile, but kind of toned down. Jake shifted his helmet to his left hand and extended his right hand to Melissa. She hesitated, looked at his outstretched hand, then lifted her left hand and shook his. Left-handed, he guessed.

"Hi, Jake. I've heard all about you from Nancy," she said.

Not again, Jake thought. "Hi, Mel—um, Melissa. Susanna didn't tell us she had a twin. So I'm sorry if I looked surprised." And sorry I stared at your scar like a rude idiot, he thought. "Jarrad and Peter will be down soon."

"Melissa is also being considered as a junior guide," Nancy said. "She couldn't join us until today 'cause she had a couple of mountainboard races. She used to be top-ranked boardercross girl in the U.S., you know."

"That was last year," Melissa corrected Nancy, shifting her pretty blue eyes briefly towards the ground.

"Yes, that's what I meant," Nancy said hurriedly. "We're really happy to have you join us this trip,

Melissa. Sam even started cheering when your dad said you'd come."

"Thanks," Melissa mumbled with a shy smile.

"So Jake," Nancy continued, "if Peter and Jarrad are just behind you, I'll put the soup on to boil for an early lunch."

Jake nodded as Nancy moved away. He remembered now that Nancy had said two girls would be joining them, but no one had ever said the word "twins," and given that no one had mentioned anything about the second girl since, he and Peter had pretty much forgotten.

He wondered why Melissa had been top-ranked last year and not this year. Must've had some kind of crash, judging from that scar. Maybe the crash had made her a little less go-for-it. But top ranked was pretty impressive.

"Well, welcome Melissa," Jake said, his voice cracking with its usual rotten timing. His face went hot.

"Blueberries," Melissa said, pointing to his helmet. "You picked some berries on the way down."

"Either that or he scrambled his brains during a fall and they spilled out blue," Susanna joked, grabbing Jake's helmet from him and stepping over to the camp's kitchen area to select a bowl.

Jake was unable to look directly at this new Melissa, and not just because of her face scar; he always went all awkward when confronted with a girl to whom he felt instantly attracted. He found himself gazing at the ground. From the corner of his eye, he saw the girl fold her gloved hands together as if she was a little nervous too.

"Hey," he said, forcing himself to look up at those familiar but not familiar long-lashed eyes, "you still have your gloves on."

There followed an awkward silence as Melissa slowly unfolded her hands.

"I always wear gloves," she said hesitantly, darting a look at her twin.

"Oh," Jake said stupidly, wondering what he'd said wrong. He reached to the ground for his water bottle, feeling like he needed a drink.

Melissa smiled at him—that heart-stopping smile he'd almost managed to make himself immune from in Susanna—and lifted her right gloved hand in front of his face. She seemed to be struggling to make a decision. Then she held his eyes firmly and whipped off her glove. There was nothing there. Her arm ended at her wrist.

Jake couldn't help staring, but he kept himself from stepping back or dropping his water bottle.

Holding Jake's eyes in a brave, defiant manner, Melissa rolled up her shirt sleeve to reveal a stump above where her hand should be. An angry, scarred stump matching the hardened skin on one side of her face. No wonder she wore long sleeves and gloves even on a hot day. And she wasn't necessarily left-handed; she just couldn't do a handshake with the right.

"This is my best boarding arm," she said as her sister rejoined them. Her eyes remained defiant. "Works like a secret weapon when I'm crouched down and power-sliding through a turn."

"Secret weapon's a good term," Susanna spoke up, grinning as she draped an arm protectively around her sister's shoulders again. "No one messes with my sister and her wicked stump when she's bombing a hill." The blonde sisters smiled at each other, then at Jake.

Jake, knowing that "bombing" meant coming down real fast, smiled back a little weakly. With the hand not holding his water bottle, he gripped the end of his mountainboard as if needing to lean on it for support. Just looking at her, he felt like the needle on his compass doing a confused 720 spin. Given her resemblance to Susanna, he also felt as if he was looking into a trick mirror.

"Ouch!" Nancy shouted just then from the camp stove.

The girls spun around. Jake, sensing trouble, sprinted toward his boss. She was holding up a reddened arm; beside her sandaled feet was a patch of mud where the boiling pot on the campstove had obviously splashed some soup onto the dry ground.

"I've burned myself!" Nancy said, gripping the arm with the opposite hand, teeth gritted. She turned toward the pot as if she couldn't believe it.

"Cold water! You need cold water!" Jake said, dropping his mountainboard from one hand to unscrew the cover of his water bottle so he could direct it onto her burn.

"Aiyee!" Nancy screamed as Jake's falling mountainboard crashed against the stove and tipped what was left of the boiling soup toward her bare legs. She leapt out of the way just in time.

"Nancy!" Jarrad's shout came from behind them as he boarded into camp at high speed. He released himself from his board in one quick downward swoop and stepped off beside the group, Peter not far behind. Jarrad stared wide-eyed at Nancy, then at Jake, seemingly unfazed by the presence of the twins. Then his accusing eyes moved to Jake's guilty face as Nancy's own eyes struggled to hide a flash of anger.

Jake was now all too aware of five sets of eyes on him. He also registered that Susanna had stepped protectively in front of Melissa. Everyone was overreacting, Jake thought sullenly, moving his board out of the way and reaching for the first-aid kit.

"Sorry, Nancy, sorry," he mumbled, realizing that he'd just flunked yet again, so to speak, in front of everyone.

"No biggie," Nancy said, allowing him to apply cold water, then ointment to her arm's minor burn. "It mostly missed, luckily, and there're lots more packets of soup. My fault, really." Her eyes were friendly again, fond. She even chuckled. "Showing off your first-aid skills, eh? There's our top junior guide."

Jake's face went hot. He dared not look at Peter's face, which he imagined to be stormy for a second. He did glance quickly at Jarrad, only to see the new senior guide's eyes narrow.

"So," Nancy said as Jake finished and packed away the first-aid kit. "Peter, you need to meet Melissa, Susanna's twin sister."

Jake turned to see Peter looking from one to the other with the same startled look at Melissa's scarred face. She'd pulled her glove back on to hide the stump, Jake noticed, and was surveying Peter cautiously.

"Okay, so I wasn't seeing double," Peter said, pumping the gloved left hand that Melissa finally held out to him. "Nice to meet you, Melissa. Susanna, you little sneak, you didn't tell us she was arriving today or that she was an identical twin. In fact, I forgot all about your having a sister joining us!"

"Well, we're pleased to have her here. Sam sure spent lots of time talking your dad into letting you come," Nancy addressed Melissa as she tore open a new envelope of soup mix. "How'd things go today, Jarrad?"

"Good-o. And g'day, Melissa. About time we put a face to a phone voice. Glad you could make it," he added curtly with no trace of surprise about Melissa's facial scar as he swapped his helmet for his leather hat.

"All three of these nippers are hot to trot," he continued, addressing Nancy. "At least, they will be with a little more coaching. Two more mountains and I'll have 'em whipped into shape. That's no bull, Nance. You can tell Sam it's going fine."

Nippers, Jake thought. Interesting how he calls us "galas," as in idiots, only when "Nance" can't hear him. Seems like he acts one way when she's around, and another way when she's not. Wonder if there's an Aussie expression for "two-faced"? A chameleon, maybe?

"Perfect," Nancy said as she stirred the soup.

"Nancy," Peter spoke up. "Jarrad and I have been debating something, and we need your opinion on which of us is right."

Jake noticed Jarrad's frown, like the senior guide wasn't interested in Nancy knowing whatever he and Peter had been arguing about.

"Yes?" Nancy replied, eyeing Jarrad.

"Jarrad thinks guides should learn just by doing, and I think it's important for guides to read books, too. On survival and weather and first aid and whatever, as part of their training. Makes them better guides, right? I think the best guides need brains and book training, not just experience, know what I'm saying?"

She took her time, looking up from the newly steaming pot. "The best guides, Peter, know their sport, the outdoors, and first aid. They're also good with people. Doesn't matter whether it's experience or books that gets them there. Okay?"

Peter nodded and refrained from replying or looking at Jarrad. But Jake knew him well enough to see that his buddy felt as if he'd been shot down.

Nancy turned off the stove, ladled up the soup, and pointed everyone to the picnic table. When everyone was seated and making short work of the soup, she stood at the head of the table, clutching her clipboard against her chest. "Now that we're all gathered, I think it's time to make my surprise announcement."

Surprise announcement? Jake tensed up as everyone looked at Nancy.

"Unlike other guide training trips, I'm not going to be around on this one any more. As you know, I don't mountainboard, so I'm leaving you entirely in Jarrad's hands for the next nine days. You've got three days on each of the three mountains to get to know the trails before the client trips begin. That," she looked meaningfully at Jarrad, "gives you eight more days to come up to Jarrad's standards. I'll see you at the end of that. Good luck."

The last two words came out stiffly, Jake thought. He took a deep breath as she smiled formally at each of them in turn—half-avoiding Jake's eyes, unless he was imagining that. Then she handed her clipboard and set of minibus keys to Jarrad. Jarrad calmly clipped the keys onto his rabbit's-foot key ring and gripped the clipboard firmly in his big hands. He looked around the stunned group and smiled. A different smile, Jake thought. A sort of triumphant, evil-looking sneer.

"So, mates," Jarrad said, rising from the table, his hard face darkly shadowed by his hat brim. "Like Nance said, I'm it now. And sure as the Australian sun sets red, there'll be no slacking off from now on. Time to say your goodbyes to Nancy."

7 New Management

It was Day Three on Mount Hood, twenty-four hours since Angus, Nancy's boyfriend, had picked her up and taken her away. Black clouds obliterated their view of any white-capped mountains. A cool breeze hinted at an approaching storm. No birds chirped, and only the occasional squirrel skittered away from the sober chain of four junior guides marching up the steep mountain path. The mountainboard strapped to Jake's backpack creaked and shifted with each step, in time with his heavy breathing. The wheels spun and his brow dripped sweat. He raised his eyes to the dark form of Jarrad, who'd set a blistering pace ahead.

"Come on, you slackers. Put a move on, girls. It ain't gonna get any easier," their leader growled as he spun around and surveyed the line with a scowl, then resumed his unrelenting speed.

I'm in top physical condition, Jake reflected, and I can hardly keep up with Jarrad. What's with him today? Jake slowed to let his three teammates catch up. The twins, fit and determined, were putting in a heroic effort but falling behind. Peter, chatting like crazy, was walking three-abreast with the girls even when the trail narrowed to make that difficult. As they caught up with Jake, Peter spoke in a husky whisper.

"It's not fair he's making us walk up the mountain," Peter whispered, addressing both Jake and the girls. "It's stupid that he leaves the minibus just parked in camp."

"Yeah," Susanna agreed, her shoulders hunched against the dead weight of a twenty-pound board. "He could just drive us up and let us come down on our own for some of the runs."

"He should hire a local to do the driving up and down," Melissa suggested in an even quieter voice as she walked beside her sister.

"Can't believe he forced us to do two seshes yesterday after Nancy left," Peter groused. "Two three-hour walks up and two two-hour trips down."

"But it sure made Jake's chili taste good last night for supper," Melissa observed. She smiled at him, which made Jake incapable of responding.

"We barely finished before dark," Peter went on, "and he barked at us all the way, like he's a drill sergeant or something."

True enough. Jake remembered tumbling into the tent more tired than he'd ever been in his life.

"Hey, he's whipping us into shape," Jake countered with attempted cheerfulness, even while wondering if a hot spot on his heel might be a developing blister. "It's a test. And hiking up lets us scout."

"Scouting's only useful on the first trek up," Melissa responded, smirking while accelerating her pace.

"Hey, Mel, wait for me," said Susanna, clearly out of breath.

Jake noticed they were always beside each other, whether hiking up the mountain or boarding down it—almost as if they were joined at the hip. He thought it was nice they liked each other that much, that they got along so well. Sometimes, though, he had the impression that the effervescent Susanna was sticking to the quiet Melissa more than the other way around. Was that to make sure Melissa's injuries weren't holding her back? And when was someone going to say how she got them?

"Hey, Susanna, come look at this," Peter said, pointing to something on the path beside his feet. "Elk droppings. Wouldn't it be cool to see some elk up here?"

Susanna, between huffs, gave him her one thousand watt smile, but said, "Sorry, Peter. I can't talk and keep up with Mel."

Jake couldn't help smiling. Peter's efforts to separate those two so that he could talk at Susanna and maybe impress her with stuff gleaned from his books wasn't working.

Undeterred, Peter hustled to walk beside the twins again. "Did you hear about the elk herd that got flash-fried on Mount St. Helens when it erupted in 1980? They were still standing there like stuffed deer, hooves in the cooling ash, when forest rangers got to the site. But when the rangers touched the elk, the elk collapsed into piles of ash, every one of them."

Jake noticed Susanna throw a worried glance at Melissa, as if concerned her sister might find that information too disturbing. Melissa appeared to be studiously ignoring Peter and his never-ending talking. Susanna turned back to Peter with an indulgent smile. "So what other wildlife used to be up here, or maybe has come back again?"

That launched Peter into a long-winded answer as Susanna smiled and nodded her head, encouraging him and his know-it-all manner.

"Come on, you drongos, move it." Jarrad's voice boomed out unexpectedly, causing Jake to jump. Drongos, Jake thought ruefully. How many words for "idiots" does Australian slang have?

"Especially you two earbashers," Jarrad added, pointing to Peter and Susanna without a hint of humor. Jake found himself exchanging bemused smiles with Melissa. Peter and Susanna were both motormouths, no denying it. Now Jake had a new word for it.

"We're keeping up fine, Jarrad," Peter objected in a polite tone. "Hey, look out for the poison oak on the left. We sure don't want anyone taking a fall in that patch, hey? Something to point out to the clients."

Jarrad halted and swung fully around. A low rumble of thunder signaled that the storm wasn't far away. Jarrad's eyes looked like an early flash of lightning. "You're not impressing anyone, least of all me, Peter. So shut your trap and leave the nerdy stuff back in the tent—or you won't be around to be telling clients anything. Got the message?"

Jake took a deep breath and dared a sideways glance at Peter's face. His buddy looked stunned, his face flushed. Peter set his jaw, looked meaningfully at Jake, and waited till Jarrad was out of earshot before whispering, "Maybe Jarrad's descended from an escaped convict. Australia is where the English sent their rottenest prisoners, you know. That's how Australia was founded."

Susanna giggled; Melissa frowned and put those new boarding shoes into faster motion. Jake slowed to walk beside Peter. "It's a test, Peter. Stay focused."

A test that Nancy surely hadn't ordered, had she?

She'd left them in the hands of a senior guide who'd been polite and enthusiastic when she was around. Did she know about his dark side? Did Sam?

Another rumble of thunder was accompanied by a spatter of rain.

"You sure we want to board down in the rain?" Jake dared to ask Jarrad. Riding down muddy trails was a wack idea.

Jarrad whirled around and studied Jake as if he was a kindergarten kid who'd just staged a temper tantrum. "This is the Northwest. Rain happens. This storm's gonna move around us. But I'll tolerate no softies or flunkies on this trip, be they Nancy's favorites or not."

Whoa. Jake felt the breath go out of him. Where had that come from and what had he done to deserve it? He gritted his teeth and reminded himself, "This is a test."

The spatters were large and cold, like slaps in the face. They lasted long enough to dampen clothing and shut down conversation. But as often happens with mountain weather, the storm moved on to dump the majority of its wrath somewhere else before the mountainboarders arrived at their takeoff point.

"Peter, you take the lead," Jarrad commanded. "Jake, you're second. You two have to learn to call and signal each other if there's trouble on the steep sections. Girls, you go after them. Put more room between the two of you this time, but stay within earshot. Mel, you go last so I can tell you what you're doing wrong."

What about what she's doing right? Jake wondered. *She's an amazing boarder, especially considering her disability.*

They set off in the order specified, with half-hearted conversation breaking the silence. They warmed up by traversing back and forth across the wide path, controlling their speed by turning and reading the terrain. Jake was well aware that sand, loose dirt, and long grass could be used to slow down—but stopping too fast could mess you up big time.

"When you're speeding, keep your body over your back wheels and use your front foot to control the carving," Jarrad reminded them loudly.

As if we don't know that, Jake thought.

"Lean into your turns using your toes or heels to initiate a turn."

Does he think he's teaching beginners or training junior guides? Jake wondered grumpily. Embarrassingly, however, on Jake's first turn, his front wheels slid out on him.

"Jake!" Jarrad called out. "Keep your weight more evenly balanced and use your back foot to push out into loose dirt!"

"Okay," Jake agreed aloud, hoping Jarrad would pick on someone else next. This wasn't the cheerful storytelling and singing Jarrad of a few days ago.

"Peter, do a rail-grab for us," Jarrad yelled toward the front of the group.

Jake watched Peter lower himself to a crouch, grab the board's toeside rail with his leading hand, lean back sharply, and put his board into a backhand power slide. Everyone followed suit, sliding into the loose dirt to avoid crashing into or overtaking him.

"Mate! You didn't kick the board up enough!" Jarrad ruled, even though Jake thought Peter had shown real style. "Get lower down, lean back, and put more power into your power turns."

His commando voice took only the briefest rest. "Okay, carve it up, kids. Keep your eyes ahead on the trail."

Why? Jake thought. We've done this trail so many times already I could about do it in my sleep. In fact, I'm starting to do it in my sleep.

Their new boss had given them barely a breather between the climb up and his orders to head down. Over the next hour, Jarrad had them switch positions as if they were soldiers on rotating watch duty. It was while Jake was up front and carving nice, wide turns that he let his eyes slip off the trail for only a second. Thump! He hit an unidentified object with his front truck.

All his board's momentum transferred itself to him, turning him into a projectile that could stop only by landing like a rag doll. His feet came out of his bindings and his board went soaring in another direction. He rolled over and over on hard dirt, hitting rocks and tree roots until the branches of a downed tree brought him to an abrupt halt.

Jake rolled into a ball, groaning and half expecting the rest of the team to land on him. He heard the crash of boards and people as a traffic pileup ensued. He heard some screams, and he heard a deep Aussie voice bellowing expletives to which no Sam's Adventure Tours sign-up should ever be subjected.

"Wasn't … my … fault," Jake moaned through a grimace. "My board tripped over nothing."

The "nothing," he determined after he'd examined new bloody wounds up his right arm, leg, and back, turned out to be a snake beside a loose rock. At least it hadn't bitten him.

"A western rattlesnake, the only poisonous snake up here," Peter identified, peering at what was left of its mangled carcass.

Jarrad sprinted from one fallen boarder to another, checking out the carnage and doling out antiseptic wipes and bandages from his first-aid kit. Doing triage, Jake reflected humorlessly. Luckily, no one had broken or punctured anything vital. The falls had just taken the scabs off the top layer of prior road-rash wounds.

Jake watched Jarrad lean over the snake carcass, pull his knife from its sheath, and slice the rattle off the end of its tail. He held it up for inspection, then stuck the grisly souvenir in his pocket. Finally, he stepped on the flattened snake like a cowboy who comes across them every day.

"What did I say about the leader needing to keep his eyes glued on the trail ahead?" Jarrad launched into the lecture Jake knew he had coming. "You thought you knew the trail by now, didn't you, Jake? But you've learned the hard way that new obstructions can appear even on a trail you've done an hour before. Every one of your mates' road rash is your fault," he continued, the index finger of a dirt-caked glove pointing at Jake as Jake rose. "Everyone went down but Melissa and me."

Jake glanced up the trail to see a strange line in the dirt on the side of the trail, as if someone had dragged a log down it. Melissa, he realized. Her "secret weapon" brake. Her stump.

"Anyone could've hit a snake the same color as the trail," Melissa challenged Jarrad. She sent what was left of the snake into the nearby forest with one swift kick from her boarding shoes. Then she pulled her filthy right glove further up on the arm missing a hand and tightened the Velcro strap that kept it on.

"Wrong, girl. No one"—Jarrad paused for effect—"can afford to miss seeing something that can turn a flowing line into a disaster scene. I would think you more than anyone, Mel, would want to avoid more injuries."

Melissa stared at him, jaw a bit ajar.

"Hey, girl," he added with an unexpected smile, "your dad felt this training would be good for you—once Sam convinced him, anyway. So do I. But don't expect any breaks from me. I'm not that kind of guy. So what if your dad and Sam are buddy-buddies?" He half-snorted before carrying on, and Jake thought he could hear Susanna draw in her breath. "You gotta have the right stuff to be a mountainboard guide with this company. You're good and you know it. But you gotta learn to stand up to people since your accident, stand up for yourself. You'll thank me one of these days."

"Fat chance," Jake heard Mel say under her breath, so quietly that their harsh guide couldn't hear her.

Jake gritted his teeth, hating Jarrad just then but willing Mel not to back-sass the Convict, as Peter had begun calling their leader. Still, he was half-surprised when she didn't. He looked up, curious to see Melissa's dismayed eyes locked instead on the dusty rabbit's-foot key ring that had fallen out of Jarrad's shorts pocket.

Jarrad leaned down to retrieve it. "Let's get moving," he commanded. "Melissa up front, Jake in the back so I can tell him what he's doing wrong."

What I'm doing wrong, Jake thought bitterly, is working for Sam's Adventure Tours on this brutal training trip.

8 Campfire

Peter was glad when Jarrad turned in early that night—crawled into his tent with a lantern and his clipboard—leaving the teens to hang out around the campsite out of his hearing.

It had been a tough day, what with Jarrad's unexpectedly ugly mood. Peter felt like last week's Jarrad had left the country and a new one had taken his place. Worse, Susanna was acting differently since Melissa had shown up. She seemed more into Mel than she was into him. In fact, she hardly ever left Mel's side. On the trail, it was obviously because Mel was hesitant at times. She fell now and then, like someone slightly rusty, someone just getting back into the sport after being away from it for a bit. But why would Susanna be protective of her off the trail, like right now? Mel seemed to twitch every time the campfire crackled loudly or sent out a spark. And every time Mel twitched, Susanna would grasp her sister's hand or lean in to whisper to her.

"Hey girls, come closer to the fire," he said, tossing a fresh log on. "Gets kind of cool here at night, don't you think?"

He turned to see Mel draw her knees up to her face and clutch her dusty boarding shoes, and Susanna squeeze her sister's shoulder as if to comfort her.

"Maybe when the fire burns down a little," Susanna said. "It's a little too hot at the moment." She was looking at Mel as she said it, the way a mom might look at a frightened little girl.

Peter glanced at Jake, who was sitting quietly on the next log, seemingly mesmerized by the dancing flames.

"No problem," Peter said. He used a big stick to poke and prod the fire until he'd managed to roll a half-charred log out, collapsing the fire into a smaller one. Jake looked up quizzically.

Peter turned around. The girls hadn't moved an inch. He shrugged, walked away from the fire, and plopped himself down beside Susanna. From that angle, given the shadows and the faraway glow of the flickering flames, he couldn't see the bad side of Mel's face. Seemed like he was sitting next to two Susannas.

Jake was looking uncertainly toward them, as if he needed an invitation to join Peter and the girls. Poor

Jake. Way too shy around the female species. All the more for me, Peter mused with a grin.

"Hey, Mel," Peter said as he watched Jake poke the fire with a long stick. "How about you go look after Jake? He's playing with fire."

Mel turned to give him a look he couldn't interpret, but it had a hint of anger. Strange girl. Then Susanna gave him the same look. For what? Okay, so they weren't into campfires. No biggie. More romantic in the shadows back here.

"You cold, Susanna?" Peter asked. "Want my fleece jacket? I'm too warm." She was wearing a thin white blouse over a lavender camisole, and her jean skirt. He was pleased when she accepted the fleece. "Jake," he called out at his brooding friend. "The party's back here, old buddy."

Jake dropped the stick he was playing with and strode back to the threesome, sitting awkwardly a few feet away from Mel. He looked as if he thought she was going to bite him or something. If Peter could get Jake and Mel together, maybe Susanna wouldn't be so into "babysitting" her sister. Jake could do whatever watching over Mel that Susanna seemed to think was necessary. Susanna probably just didn't want her sis to get any more scars, that was it.

"Hey Jake, I think we need more water. It's your and Mel's turn to collect it, right?"

Jake nodded and stood up. Such a sucker, Peter thought with a smirk. The smirk broadened into a smile as Mel stood to follow Jake and his flashlight into the darkened woods.

"So, ask me anything about Mount Hood National Park, and see if I know the answer," Peter challenged Susanna, sidling a few inches closer to her.

She giggled a real girl-giggle, music to his ears. "Okay, what kind of bird is making that 'peent, peent' sound somewhere near us?" Susanna asked with a smile. "I thought birds slept at night."

"Aha, they usually do. But not the nighthawk," Peter replied, squinting uselessly into the darkness. "Neither do spotted owls, and it'd be way cool if we heard or saw one of those. They're around here, but they're an endangered species."

"Okay, and what do you make of the radio reports that say Mount St. Helens sent up some smoke today? Think it's getting ready to blow again? Mel and I don't want to board over there if it is."

Peter turned to survey Susanna's beautiful face in the flickering firelight. It looked kind of serious. "St. Helens puffs now and then. It's totally normal. She's just venting a little, kind of like Jarrad today, hey? What's with him, do you think?"

She shrugged with relaxed shoulders and pulled his fleece tighter around her. "Bad mood for a day. I guess. Or just letting us know he's the new boss. He can't say anything bad about you, though. You were, like, awesome today on your board."

"Thanks!" he said. "You were looking pretty together yourself. So how long have you and Mel been boarding?"

"Coupla years," she replied. "Mel was always better than me. She's still amazing, but just been away from it for a little while. Just wait and see her by the end of this trip."

"She was starting to flow by the end of the day. She seems stoked to be here. And how about you?" He moved another inch closer.

"I'm okay," she said a little hesitantly. "Mel's really into being hired as a guide, you know. She figures it'll prove she can board as well as … um, as well as before the accident … when she lost her hand. And Sam, your boss, was really leaning on Dad to sign her up. He kept going on about using girl mountainboarding guides to get more girl clients to sign up. He's pretty obsessed with that, isn't he?"

"Dunno," Peter said. "He only mentioned it once when Jake and I were around. Anyway, we mostly work with Nancy. Don't deal with Sam that much. Been working with Nancy for years. Doing all the sports, not just mountainboarding."

"Mmmm," Susanna replied slightly uneasily. "Well,

Sam told Dad we'd just be doing the mountainboarding trips. If," she added hastily, "he ends up hiring Mel—I mean us—at all. Mel's gotta prove she's got all her speed and confidence back since her accident."

Peter was dying to ask what kind of accident, but he figured he should wait until one of the twins volunteered the information. He had a feeling that Susanna might be impressed if he didn't follow that up right away.

"Good. And you want to guide for Sam's Adventure Tours too?"

She sighed and looked down. "Maybe," she said uncertainly. "Jarrad told me I have the skills. But really I just thought it'd be fun to come on this trip. And ... and once Mel started begging my parents to let her do this, my parents decided she could come only if I came along too."

"I see," Peter said. "Not much fun today, was it? But Jarrad was really cool before Nancy left. So I figure he'll mellow out and be okay again."

"You like being a junior guide?" Susanna asked, shivering and fiddling with the unzipped zipper on the coat.

Peter leaned over and zipped it up for her, boldly lifting her golden hair up and out of the way while he was at it. "Love it," Peter said. Then he sighed. "Love it, but my parents say it's a waste of time. That I should be doing summer school my last few summers before college, because 'it doesn't take many brains to be a guide, and you need something intellectual to help you get into college.'" He uttered the sentence with a nasally tone, prompting her to laugh as he'd hoped.

He frowned again. "My parents say this will be my last trip with Sam's," he said, dropping his elbows to his knees as they sat on the log, and scowling. "But I have a plan."

"A plan?" Susanna asked, her glowing face moving toward his.

"Yes. If I can impress Jarrad on this trip, and get him and Nancy and Sam to convince my parents that it does take brains to guide—that we learn lots of intellectual stuff—then maybe they'll let me keep being a guide on my summer vacations. I mean, even businesses send employees on wilderness adventures to make them better leaders or 'team players.'"

"Hmmm," Susanna said, nodding encouragingly. "Sounds like a sensible plan."

He hoped so. He really hoped so. He had only nine days to do it, including getting through all the books he'd hauled along. Just as he lifted his face to Susanna in an effort to gauge her interest in him, Jake and Mel reappeared, each weighed down with a bucket of water. Peter watched Mel as she made a wide berth around the fire. She was still wearing her bike gloves.

He'd never seen her without them. He had yet to see the stump that one of the gloves was hiding, but Jake had told him about it.

Guess Melissa's just not used to campfires or something. Or she's nervous of fires? But she seemed so outdoorsy otherwise. That didn't fit.

"You know, I'm pretty tired," Melissa confessed as she and Jake drew close to Susanna and Peter. "I think I'm going to call it a night and go crawl into the tent."

Peter didn't like it one bit when that made Susanna stand up, stretch, and yawn. "Me, too," she said casually. "We probably all need a good night's sleep to handle whatever the Convict has in store for tomorrow." She giggled and turned to Peter. "Good name, Peter."

"Thanks!" Peter replied brightly.

"Tomorrow's Mount Adams," Jake reminded them. "Tougher trails. It's higher and steeper than Hood."

"St. Helens is the lowest of the three," Peter inserted. "It was even before it blew its top."

"Could blow again anytime, the news was saying today," Jake said. "Maybe that part of our trip will get canceled."

"Nah, the news just said they're monitoring it real closely," Peter said, accepting his fleece as Susanna took it off and handed it back to him. "They'll close the park if things look serious. But I doubt that'll happen. Helens has spouted ash tons of times since the big eruption. Doesn't mean another big blowout is coming."

"Maybe so, but officials didn't close off enough areas back in 1980," Melissa spoke up. "That's why people got killed."

"Fifty-five of them," Peter agreed. "Not to mention 200 bears, 6,000 deer, 5,000 elk, and 100 mountain goats. But you can't blame anyone. The scientists keep saying they don't know enough to make exact predictions."

"True," Melissa said, taking a step toward her and Susanna's tent. "Don't forget to drown the fire before you guys turn in." She threw a concerned look at the dying embers, which she never did sit close to the entire night, Peter reflected. "Good night."

"Melissa definitely doesn't like campfires," Jake mused quietly to Peter after the girls had gone.

"Scared of fire, you think?" Peter responded. "Hey, maybe her accident had something to do with fire? Fire can scar a person."

"Now that would make sense," Jake said, nodding. "Wish someone would tell us what happened to her, but I don't like to ask."

Peter and Jake looked at each other, shrugged, and kicked dirt on the fire till its last glowing coals died.

"What do you make of Jarrad being so mean today?" Peter asked Jake in a low voice.

Jake heaved a sigh. "Kind of weird, eh? Like he thinks he has to show us he's in charge now. Or maybe it was just a bad mood for a day. Tomorrow'll be better."

Peter nodded and followed Jake to their tent. Poor Jake was probably thinking about the snake collision. That sure hadn't impressed the Convict. But Jake didn't need to impress anyone at Sam's. He was their darling. No, Peter, he scolded himself, stop thinking like that. If Jarrad is going to make things tough on us, it's important for all us junior guides to work as a team. We just have to cooperate and do our best and stay positive, he instructed himself. That's what would impress Jarrad.

That, and Peter knowing lots of facts about the region, facts that clients would get a kick out of hearing. Trivia like how most of the people got killed on St. Helens: from breathing in ash, or from the snow melting and turning into major mudflows, or just from being too close to the heat. Not like Pompeii, Italy, two thousand years ago, where the whole city got buried by ash and cinders. He also knew what kinds of trees grew in the western Cascade mountains: western red cedar, Douglas fir, and western hemlock. And what animals clients might see: bears, coyotes, wolverines, pikas, gophers—

"'Night," Jake said loudly, elbowing his tent mate as Peter lay in his sleeping bag, his flashlight trained on one of his guidebooks.

"Yeah, all right," he agreed, placing the book carefully in his stack and switching off the flashlight.

9 Mount Adams

Jake and Mel were the first ones up. As they busied themselves with camp chores, Jake searched for some way to start a conversation, a way to get to know her better.

"So you and Susanna are keen to be junior guides?" he asked.

She smiled brightly. "I am. I really am. I think Susanna's just along for fun."

"But why would Sam let someone come along just for fun? I mean, he's paying our food and everything."

She was quiet, her eyes on the forest floor for a moment.

"Sam wanted me to come 'cause of my racing name and experience and all. Dad wouldn't let me come without Susanna. He's been kind of overprotective of me ever since my accident. Dad and Sam are good friends, so they worked it out. That's all I know about it. I don't know how much Nancy or Jarrad knows about that, but it's the truth. Anyway, now that we're here, Susanna is enjoying herself, maybe even getting more interested in the whole thing. She's a good boarder," Mel added in a defensive tone.

"Fair enough," Jake said, raising an eyebrow at this inside information, but somehow not shocked by it. "You know, you're boarding better every day, and you work hard in camp. If you want to make sure you get hired, my advice is to ignore Jarrad's insults. Not easy, I know, but he's got a lot of experience and we need to pretend his mean comments roll right off us."

She nodded. "You're right. Especially about the not-easy part. I figure if I want to be a guide for Sam, I also have to watch you—try and be like you, 'cause Nancy told me you're the company's best junior guide."

Jake blushed deeply. How dare Nancy say that to Mel!

"She's thinking of some of my other sports, not mountainboarding. Anyway, I doubt she thinks that any more, the way I've been messing up. She told me a few weeks ago that I'm acting like I'm burned out. I got really mad when she said that. I argued there's no way. But lately I've been wondering." He shrugged, feeling miserable. "I've never blown things as much as I have this last week. And I hate people saying Nancy likes me better than anyone else."

He said it with more emotion than he'd meant to. Mel studied him for a few seconds. Then in a shy, quiet voice she said, "You've been a junior guide a long time, Jake. Maybe you're ready to move on, do something else? Maybe Nancy liking you so much makes that hard? I mean," she said hurriedly, "that's what happens to me when I'm split in two about something; I start messing up half on purpose without even realizing I'm doing it."

Jake felt his teeth clench. How dare she! But before he had a chance to answer, Peter crawled out of their tent, leaving Jake feeling annoyed as well as mortified and wondering whether he'd overheard any of their conversation.

"When's Jarrad getting up?" Peter asked groggily. "Isn't he supposed to be our leader, kicking us out of bed early?"

"He likes his sleep. We've had to wake him up every morning so far," Jake reminded Peter.

"Jarrad! We're all up and waiting for you for breakfast!" Jake and Peter shouted, one after the other.

Twenty minutes later, as the four trainees and their sleepy guide ate porridge, Jake felt relaxed again; he was wiping the memory of Mel's comments clear out of his mind. He put a finger to his lips and pointed to a clump of bushes up the hill. The others followed his eyes. Jake heard a small exclamation of delight from

Melissa. It was a rabbit, a wild hare, nose twitching and big eyes alert as it nibbled on some grass.

"It's so cute," Melissa murmured, her gloves clasped together, her eyes alight.

"It's wild," Susanna spoke up. Jake thought it odd that her tone smacked of a warning or scolding.

The rabbit, soon joined cautiously by a second one in the upper clearing, continued nibbling, standing sentry, and nibbling some more.

"Wish I had my twelve-gauge shotgun," a deep voice rumbled from beside them. "It'd be awesome to have some rabbit stew tonight."

Was that comment meant to tease the girls, or was he itching to shoot the rabbits for real? For real, Jake decided.

"I hunt 'em back home. You have to hit 'em in the eyes so you don't get any lead shot in 'em. I could skin and gut those two in sixty seconds," he boasted, pulling his knife out of its sheath and twirling its tip on a calloused thumb as the blade glinted in the morning sunlight.

"This is a national park," Melissa's steady, angry voice responded, her eyes locking with Jarrad's. "You don't have to kill everything you're around, Jarrad."

Jarrad squinted at her quizzically, then pulled his rabbit's foot key ring out of his pocket and fondled it as if it were a proud possession. "A double-barreled twelve-bore" was all he replied, his voice wistful.

To Jake's surprise, Melissa leapt up and strode over to her tent, her skater shoes leaving firm imprints in the dirt, her remaining porridge left to turn cold.

Two seconds of silence later, Susanna rose and walked to the tent, where hushed voices were heard arguing, comforting.

So Jarrad was going to be flinty again today, Jake judged with an inner sigh. As the rabbits hopped away, Jake decided he liked discovering that Mel had a soft spot for wild creatures. It made her more attractive.

He was definitely attracted to Melissa. He liked her gutsiness, her intense ambition to improve herself on her mountainboard, and her quieter and more practical personality when compared with her sister's. He respected her, he was drawn to her, but he was also a little afraid of her not having a similar interest in him. He was in no hurry; he'd just watch her, get to know her, be alert for any signals, and wait for an opportunity.

"So, we move over to Mount Adams today," Peter said.

"That's right. Are you going to tell us something about Mount Adams?" Jarrad asked as he boiled water for dishwashing.

Jake caught the sarcasm in Jarrad's voice, but Peter evidently didn't.

"Yup. It's where an outlaw named J. B. Cooper

parachuted out of a hijacked 727 with $200,000 in cash in 1971. And he's never been seen since."

"You don't say. Girls!" Jarrad yelled toward the twins' tent. "Get out here and do dishes, or we're not going to get to Mount Adams in time to collect $200,000!"

The girls stuck their heads out and looked quizzically at him, then at one another. They made an amusing sight, two almost-identical blonde heads poking out of a tiny dome tent, like a two-headed snail.

"Some of the money turned up," Peter informed them. "A little girl digging in the sand along the Columbia River found a bag with around $6,000 in it. But that's all anyone's ever found."

"Hooley dooley! Well, we'll keep our eyes peeled on the trail for any bumps that look like sacks of big-bikkies—that means lots of money—left by someone who did a blow through," Jarrad stated. "Now get off your dots and help pack up camp, kids."

Nobody needed to be asked twice.

"It's also Sasquatch country," Peter informed them an hour later as they were riding in the minibus to their campsite on Mount Adams.

"You mean Bigfoot—the half-ape/half-man?" Mel asked.

"Yup. They found a body print of him in the mud up there a few years back."

"Hmmm. I bet some of you are going to make body prints in the mud today. We're going to speed things up, see how fast you can slalom down this trail," Jarrad advised them.

True to his word, Jarrad had them wired going down a new, steeper trail at a heart-stopping rate not long after they'd set up camp. But Jake didn't mind. He loved the feel of the breeze on his body, the sun on his face, the rhythm of swaying his lower body back and forth like a surfer on an ocean wave. Far beneath them, the wide Columbia River and its morning bevy of windsurfers winked.

"Mel, you've got to stay focused on the trail!" Jarrad growled. "Go left and start carving, you slacker. It's getting steeper here!"

Jake couldn't figure out why Jarrad had turned both rancorous and remote. Why did he feel a need to spoil such a great day and sweet trail? But already, the team seemed to be adjusting to their surly leader, as if the Jarrad Jake thought he remembered from a few days ago had never existed. Jake could see, could almost feel, the way Mel gritted her teeth every time Jarrad criticized her. But she seemed to suck up her anger at his tone and insults, focusing entirely on adopting the advice in his malevolent stream of words.

She's tough, she's resilient, she's spirited, Jake thought admiringly. She'd have needed to be all that to make a comeback from the trauma of her accident. No doubt Susanna had been a big help. Susanna shadowed her sister day and night. Jake had a sister he was fond of, but they certainly didn't have that kind of closeness.

Thinking of his family reminded Jake of why he'd joined Sam's Adventures in the first place. His family needed his income, small as his earnings were. He'd always felt important contributing, but lately it felt like a burden. He rubbed his neck as he slowed on a traverse and looked out on a panoramic view of the Columbia River valley. He sighed. He checked the leash that connected his ankle with his board. A part of him wanted to cut the leash, toss the board, hike up some side road, and … and feel freedom.

"Jake Evans, what do you think you're doing?" Jarrad shouted.

Jake tightened his bindings, adjusted his leash, and pushed off down the road ahead. Time to get back to his responsibilities. Time to memorize the features of this trail so he could lead a pack of kids down it without tripping over any rattlesnakes.

"Jake, old buddy," Peter said, maneuvering his board to ride alongside Jake. "You're spaced out today. What's up?"

"Nothing," Jake said, watching Mel pull off a 180: an easy move that switched her from forward to fakie.

Peter followed his eyes. "She's improving every hour, hey? She gets it anytime Jarrad tells her something. Never seen anyone so determined. Pretty soon Susanna won't be able to keep up with her."

"They sure stick together, don't they?" Jake commented.

"Way too much. You like Mel, don't you?"

Jake hesitated, but only for a second. "Mmmm."

"That's good. That's good. I think she likes you too. But you gotta let her know, dude. Gotta move in, you know? Gotta make the first move, lay it on a little. That's what girls like."

Jake smiled. "Stick to your mountainboard coaching, Peter. I can navigate this trail on my own." I wish, he thought silently, knowing that Peter was way better at the girl thing. But Mel wasn't Peter's type. So Peter's advice might not apply to winning her. Anyway, Jake couldn't just "move in" on her, as Peter put it. He didn't have the confidence.

Peter, probably while trying to think up some annoying comeback, tumbled over a second later. He'd messed up a Back Scratcher, an intermediate trick.

"Serves you right for being a blowhard," Jarrad ruled after Peter had risen and dusted himself off.

"Jake, you did that last turn with good flow, but you need to commit yourself to really get it right."

For some reason, Jake couldn't get it together when

Jarrad was trailing him. He got nervous, regressed to novice, or acquired two left feet.

"You need more speed! Go harder!" Jarrad screamed at him a moment later. Jake pumped it and tried again, but once again he failed, falling and rolling off the trail into some gorse bushes.

He raised his head just enough to see Jarrad shaking his head in disgust, and Mel scowling at Jarrad's back.

"Jarrad," Mel said as Jarrad opened his mouth to shout at Jake again. "I've almost got that move you said Aussies call a Chicken Salad Air, but I need to know whether I'm rotating my wrist the right way."

Jake heaved a sigh and pulled himself up. He appreciated Mel taking the heat off him, especially since he could tell by the set of her shoulders that she disliked Jarrad's coaching style as much as he did.

Had it not occurred to Jarrad that they might report his negativity, his oppressive leadership style, to Nancy and Sam? They'd surely fire him on the spot. What was the point of treating four junior guides like this when he was supposed to be training them, not killing their self-confidence?

That was it, Jake thought as he stepped back onto his board and sped down the dusty trail again. The four of them would gang up and report him. They'd huddle this evening after Jarrad turned in and agree exactly how to deal with his meanness. The four had to become a tight unit, discuss how to outwit him or give him a taste of mutiny.

Jake found his board running faster and faster the more he thought about it. He pumped his board, feeling a greater sense of control with each turn. Peter had always told Jake he was a natural leader; Nancy often said the same. Time to take charge here, he decided. Bond the four of us so tightly that Jarrad won't know what he's dealing with.

"He's a top-ranked racer in Australia," Nancy had said proudly when introducing Jarrad. "And he's great with kids, right, Jarrad?"

"Love the little nippers," Jarrad had replied.

"Liar. Big-time liar," Jake said through clenched teeth.

10 United Front

"A united front," Peter echoed Jake as the four sat around a dying campfire that evening.

Jake and Peter had figured out that the girls were uncomfortable around a big fire, so they'd been making sure it had died down a lot by the time Jarrad and his clipboard disappeared into the senior guide's spacious tent. Every night after supper, Jake noticed Jarrad scribbling on that clipboard as if he was on deadline for producing a book or something. When Peter had boldly asked him what he was writing, he'd just teased "something bad about your performance on this trip."

"Good idea," Susanna spoke up. "We'll do what the Convict says during the day, cheerfully, as if we appreciate his help, even if he is a Class A jerk."

"But keep a notebook on him like he's keeping that clipboard on us," Mel suggested, winking at Jake. His pulse soared. Had she really winked at him? "Record the way he's treating us. For Nancy and Sam."

"Perfect," Peter said.

"So every night, we'll meet like this and pool our complaints, and you're going to start the list in a notebook, Mel?" Jake asked, his voice cracking on her name.

"Sure!" she agreed enthusiastically. "It'll give me practice writing with my left hand."

She dug into her backpack and lifted out a pen in her left hand. As she did so, the right arm's empty glove fell off, exposing her stump.

Silence hung heavily as she groped to put it back on. Susanna leaned over to help her.

"Forget it," Mel muttered. She pulled back her right sleeve to expose the scarred arm and held it toward Peter, whom Jake knew had not seen it before.

"It burned off," she said suddenly—bravely, Jake thought. "My whole hand. I know you're wondering, so you might as well know."

No one said a word. Everyone's eyes were on her. Her eyes were on the glowing remains of the campfire. "Our house caught fire one night, something to do with bad wiring, they said."

"It was the middle of the night," Susanna contributed. "Mel and I had to jump out of our bedroom window on the second floor to where the firefighters were shouting at us."

“Everyone got out safely,” Mel went on, eyes reflecting the orange of the fire. “But we got out so fast we forgot my pet rabbit.”

Susanna lifted an arm and slipped it around Mel’s shoulders, which were drooping as if the story was weighing heavy on her.

“We were standing there,” Mel said, “watching it all go up in flames. Watching the big hoses shoot water at it … I wasn’t supposed to run back in, but I did it too fast for anyone to stop me.”

“I was right behind you, trying to tackle you,” Susanna reminded her.

“I got inside to where my rabbit was, and I saw her leaping around crazy-like, throwing herself against the sides of her cage. The fire was all around her.”

“You weren’t supposed to go back in the house,” Susanna said, her voice sounding defeated. She seemed to be reliving a moment that haunted her, too.

“I reached for the rabbit cage,” Mel continued as if her sister hadn’t spoken, “just as a ceiling beam came down on it.” The last words came out choked.

“And I grabbed Mel’s legs and pulled her out of the house when she started screaming. Then the firefighters leaped on her and rolled her around the ground to put out the flames on her clothes,” Susanna finished in a tired tone. “They called the ambulance. Our parents were shrieking out of control.”

Somehow, Jake didn't need to ask the fate of the rabbit.

"That's all there is to know," Mel said decisively, allowing Susanna to help her pull the empty right glove back up on her stump and Velcro it back into place on her sleeve. "I'm not going for an artificial hand or skin grafts on my face," she added firmly, touching her stump-arm to the shadowed side of her face. "People just have to accept me like I am."

Her eyes tore themselves from the campfire's ashes and lifted to Jake. They held a warmth quite apart from the dying embers, as if an inner force was fanning a growing flame. He managed to hold her eyes for a long time, his heart racing.

* * *

The next morning, Jake watched her as she boarded beside Susanna just ahead. Mel was really talented, but just slightly hesitant on any move that might knock her down onto her stump-arm. Yet even where that was an issue, she'd gained confidence over the few days he'd known her. She obviously just needed to jog her instincts back into place.

"Jake, it's your turn to lead," Jarrad barked. "And step it up so we can practice turns at high speed. Peter goes last and you two girls had better spread out some. Stop boarding so close to each other or you'll get hurt when you crash."

When you crash, not if, Jake thought darkly. Bad psychology. Something for the notebook tonight.

"Please can we board next to each other on the easier parts?" Susanna spoke up. "We pretty much know this trail by now, and you know what my dad said."

"I don't care if your parents assigned you to keep an eye on your sister," Jarrad bellowed. "There's no way she needs it. Plus it's my job when we're on the trail, isn't it?"

Jake was surprised Jarrad would shout that out publicly, making Susanna's face go beet red. And surprised to see the way Melissa drew herself up tall and shot a quick, harsh look at Susanna. Jake didn't know them well enough to interpret the glance for sure, but he'd lay his money on the notion that Melissa resented her parents assigning Susanna to serve as her guardian. She certainly seemed to have gained enough confidence the last few days to not need anyone shadowing her, especially not her twin.

"But if anything happens to her ..." Susanna protested as everyone halted their boards for a moment.

"Are you deaf, girl? I said back off the poor thing. The way you almost board on top of her, it'll be your fault anyway."

Jake and Peter exchanged looks. Who had Jarrad

enraged more with that remark, Susanna or the decidedly not "poor thing," Mel?

"Plus," Jarrad continued, jabbing a finger at Susanna as he took a step toward her, "you need to stop thinking of yourself as a babysitter. You're a mountainboarder. A darn good one whether you know it or not. So lay off Mel and start acting like a junior guide!"

None of the four teens dared speak or look at one another for a full minute after that. And even once they'd resumed boarding, Jake got a feeling something had changed. From then on, Susanna not only stopped hanging near her twin, Mel seemed to bristle anytime Susanna accidentally came within arm's reach. Hmmm, from best buddies to cranky ex-partners all at once? So much for Jake admiring their cozy sisterly closeness.

Meanwhile, Susanna—freed of her babysitting duties—transferred her full energy to Peter, chattering with him like someone who'd been starved of speaking for a week, and leaping about on her board with new confidence, gutsiness, and vivaciousness. She pulled the clasp from her hair and let it fly from under her helmet as she boarded the trail. This prompted Peter to go into his own hyper chatter-mode and to act like Jake and Mel weren't even on the trip.

Meanwhile, when Mel wasn't getting coaching from the Convict—and scribbling in a little notebook she now kept in her shorts pocket—she was talking to Jake way more. Which suited him just fine.

Late in the afternoon, maybe because she was tired, Mel failed to land something Jarrad called a Chicken Salad Air. Jake winced as gravity sent her body barrel-rolling down a steep section of the trail. He whipped his board around and sped toward her.

That's when a muffled explosion sounded from above, an explosion so loud it seemed to shake the ground beneath them. Jake froze and looked from Mel, whose mouth was now hanging open, to Jarrad, staring upslope.

"Gunshot?" Peter asked.

"Way too loud. Sounded more like a cannon," Jake declared uneasily, moving toward Mel to see if she was okay.

"Are there miners up here, maybe using dynamite?" Susanna asked.

"Plane crash?" Mel suggested, shaking a little as she struggled up and brushed herself off.

"I'd guess avalanche patrol, setting off charges in a restricted area," Jarrad said slowly, rubbing his jaw and shrugging. "Radio'll say when we get back to camp, I guess. Nothing to do with us, anyway."

"Are you okay, Mel?" Jake asked. Her fall had

bloodied an arm where it wasn't protected by gear, then coated it in dust.

"I'm fine," she said with steely resolve and a forced smile. "Hey, maybe Adams is going to blow instead of St. Helens. Maybe that was it waking up."

Jarrad rolled his eyes. "Yeah, right. No excuses. Let's get going."

Jake offered Mel his hand and helped pull her to her feet. Then she did something amazing. Instead of letting go of his hand, she held onto it, like a frightened child.

Without even thinking what he was doing, he pulled her into an embrace. For a split-second, he felt her warm lips touch his neck, as if she was grateful. As if she was letting him know she liked him. He pressed his own mouth against her neck before releasing her and pretending he was studying a new gouge on her arm. Then he fetched her runaway board for her. But really he was looking at her all the time, and she at him. Warm, knowing smiles both ways. Electricity traveled from his arms down his body right to his toes.

"Back on the trail!" the Convict shouted.

Jake looked sideways at Peter, only to see a grin and a thumb's up. So he'd seen. Or thought he had, anyway.

For the rest of the run, their boss kept urging them to go faster and faster, till all talk disappeared and full concentration went to staying on the twisting trail—and trying to take their falls in a way that minimized cuts and bruises.

Back at camp, Jarrad headed straight for the van and switched on the radio as he stared uphill again. Jake, feeling ready for a nap, sank into the nearest camp chair.

"... an unexpected tremor and burst of steam from the peak of Mount Adams this morning at 11:21," the announcer was saying. "Volcanologists stationed at Mount St. Helens are racing to Adams this afternoon to reinforce a skeleton crew on the second mountain, assumed to be dormant until this morning. Meanwhile, officials are assuring area residents that the tremor was no more than a 3.9 on the Richter scale. In a statement shortly after the mountain emitted a small amount of steam into the air, one scientist said that while Mount Adams's burst of seismic activity has caught them by surprise, there is little chance it signals an eruption in the near future, and there is no call for evacuating the area."

"Whoa! So we were right on the mountain when it erupted!" Peter exclaimed. "We, like, heard the boom and felt it go!"

"It didn't erupt, you gala," the Aussie said. "Didn't you hear what they said? A little activity, that's all. We're off of Adams tomorrow, anyway."

"Darn. It'd be way cool to board down an exploding

volcano," Peter joked, sinking into one of the camp's folding chairs.

Seeing only three chairs out, Mel perched herself boldly on Jake's knee, while Peter and Susanna sat in side-by-side chairs, holding hands.

"You four scunges need to clean yourselves up," Jarrad announced—ironic given his own personal hygiene, Jake thought, which was less than impeccable. "And fetch water and make supper. Mel doesn't have to help start the campfire, though—her parents' orders," he added, as if purposefully looking to humiliate Mel. "But before you do all that," he added, pulling his clipboard into his lap and perching on the edge of the picnic table in shorts, boots, knife belt, and outback hat, "I have an important announcement."

Jake felt himself stiffen. The last time someone with a clipboard had made an announcement, it hadn't boded well. Jake and Mel leaned in toward each other, waiting. Peter and Susanna lifted their heads Jarrad's way.

"I've been riding you hard for a couple of days, and it's time you knew why." He paused for effect. He had their undivided attention. "Sam asked me to do it. He may not have meant for me to be brutal, but he did say to push you all hard. He said Nancy is too soft on junior guides and knows them too well."

Jake frowned when Jarrad shot him a meaningful look.

"The thing is," Jarrad continued, "Sam needs only two junior guides for his mountainboarding trips this summer. Just two."

He paused. Jake and Peter looked at each other, confused. Why would Sam bring two would-be girl trainees on this trip if he needed only Jake and Peter?

"Sam has entrusted me with making the decision of which two out of you four will guide for Sam's Adventure Tours mountainboarding trips. It will be based on ability, not seniority." Here, he shot both Jake and Peter stern looks, making Jake lose his breath. Sam would consider firing him from the new mountainboarding division? Or Peter? For two girls who'd never guided for the company?

He noticed that Peter's face had gone as white as his.

"So I'll be continuing to ride you hard and rating you objectively. One more thing." Jarrad spat on the ground. "Just for the record, I hate kids."

As if we hadn't figured that out already, Jake thought bitterly.

"But if Sam wants two of you, then two of you he'll have. The best two. Get to work now."

Jarrad stood and walked to his tent with a confident stride, his black knife sheath chafing against his sunburned waist.

The four stared at one another in stunned silence, trying to take it in. Peter was the first to react. He released Susanna's hand, rose from his chair, picked up the water bucket, and headed for the stream. Mel was next. She stood up, walked to the campfire ring, and pulled the notebook out of her shorts pocket. Then she tore up some pages and sprinkled the bits onto the kindling without so much as a glance at her camp mates.

11 Competition

"He's bluffing," Peter whispered to Jake the next morning as they lay in their pup tent, freshly awake. He pulled an arm out of his sleeping bag to lift the tent flap a bit. "There's no way Sam's leaving it all up to Jarrad. He'd let Nancy have a say, too. So you're safe. Nancy would never, ever fire you, not even from just the mountainboarding trips. It's the rest of us Jarrad has forced into competition. As in, who gets voted off the … volcano?"

Peter watched Jake sit up and rub his eyes as if he was still half asleep.

"Sam doesn't have to give Nancy a say," Jake grumbled. "Sounds to me like Sam hired Jarrad so he could bypass Nancy and maybe end up with his friend's daughters. He thinks that'll increase how many girls sign up. Whatever's going on, it sucks. Jarrad's a lousy leader, and a competition is a stupid way to choose employees. This whole trip stinks, and stop saying I'm Nancy's favorite or I'll punch you. I mean that. I hate people saying that, and I don't want it to be true."

Peter sat up and stared at Jake, astonished. "Don't want it to be true? Why not? Jake, you have it all perfect! Both Sam and Nancy like you, you've been with the company forever, and your parents are totally into your being a guide." Not like my stupid, snobbish parents, he thought bitterly, who think guiding is trivial and who have dictated that this will be my last trip ever.

"My parents can't afford me not being a guide," Jake said with a weary, bitter tone that surprised Peter. Peter's eyes narrowed. "Stop being stupid, Jake. You know you're 'in.' If you were a real friend, you'd at least put in a good word for me with Jarrad. You know I want to keep guiding." He pressed his fingernails into his palms. "You have no idea how much I want to keep guiding."

Instead of agreeing with Peter, as Peter had hoped, Jake merely tossed off his sleeping bag and started pulling on clothes as if he wanted no more of the conversation. So that's how he's going to be, Peter thought, his jaw setting. He probably doesn't even want me to be the second mountainboarding guide. He's probably gunning for Mel to get it so that he and she can be an item on trips together. Well, we'll see about that. I'm going for it, and I'm not going to let anyone or anything get in my way, not even Jake. Lucky for me that Susanna isn't interested in being a guide. At least I don't have to compete with her. In fact, I have to get the slot in order to impress her. She admires the fact that I'm an experienced guide. For sure she does. So that's one more reason I have to—absolutely have to—impress Jarrad, get him to like me.

By the time Peter had scrambled out to the cooking area, Susanna was already there, her hair freshly washed in the stream and half dried in the morning sun. It looked gorgeous, golden, and thick as it fell freely all the way to the small of her back. She was wearing an electric orange muscle shirt that showed off her firm, tan shoulders, not to mention the rest of her. The smile she offered him all but convinced him to grab her and run off together right then—to forget this stupid guide-training trip. But it was just a passing thought. He gave her a quick kiss, on the lips.

"You're up early."

"I'm on breakfast duty, according to Jarrad's chart."

"Yeah, well I'll help."

"You're on water duty," came a deep, dry voice from the door of Jarrad's tent.

"Oh, right! Okay, off to the stream then!" Peter said, grabbing the bucket and walking light-footed and lighthearted out of camp. Go figure, he thought. Jarrad was actually awake already!

Butterflies fluttered amid the ferns, the blackberry bushes, and the old-growth hemlock, fir, and pine trees. Tiny birds with yellow heads—warblers—warbled from the trees in harmony with a chorus of other birds he couldn't identify. It looked—and smelled—fresh and forest-y, like an ad for air freshener.

Peter dipped the bucket into the stream, sending some tiny fish darting away. He thought how nice and pure the water looked. He glanced beside him and spotted some animal tracks, ran his brain through the pictures in one of his guidebooks to come up with what had been there: a fox. A red fox, probably scouting for Mel's rabbits. That was so horrid, the story about her hand burning off when she tried to save her pet rabbit. No wonder Susanna was protective of her injured sister. Then again, Susanna had been so much more upbeat and happy since both Jarrad and Mel had let her know to lay off doing that.

She'd turned into a whole new girl: carefree, elated, almost reckless. As if she'd been released from a cage and was going to make up for lost time. Her happiness made her glow, especially when she and Peter were together. Peter was glad for her, and more than a little proud that she was his newest girlfriend.

He peered again at the fox tracks and pictured all

the furtive creatures that visited this stream: happy in their world, their protected wilderness.

How lucky he was to get paid to visit such places! And yet, this might be his last trip ever as a guide, so it needed to be special. It already was special, what with Susanna being on it. And Jarrad might be a grouch, but already, Peter's mountainboarding skills had increased under the Convict's sharp eye and tongue.

Funny, but Peter had even gotten used to doing the long ascents with his board on his back. He could almost see the new muscles bulging in his calves, could almost feel the increased aerobic capacity in his lungs. So it was all good, right? All good for two of them by the end of the trip, anyway, he reflected with a sigh.

As he strode back into camp, he saw everyone gathered beside the minibus, listening to a radio news report.

"... coating cars this morning with a light dusting of ash. Scientists insist that these latest tremors and discharges do not constitute a need to evacuate the region. They emphasize that they're monitoring both Mount St. Helens and Mount Adams around the clock."

Jarrad switched the radio off and stared thoughtfully at each of the riders in turn.

"What did I miss?" Peter asked.

"Nothing new with Adams, but St. Helens is acting up," Jarrad said. "They've expanded the red zone, the area they won't allow anyone into. Where our trail starts is not far from the edge of the new border. I phoned Nancy and Sam, and they say it's up to me. So there's no reason we can't go ahead with driving over there tonight and mountainboarding it tomorrow. But if anyone objects, let me know now."

Everyone stared at Jarrad.

"I'm game. Just a matter of listening to the reports regularly," Peter said.

"Let's go for it," Mel said, her eyes on Susanna, challenging her.

"If we're outside the danger zone, we're fine," Susanna said, a little too cheerily.

"Whatever," Jake said casually. "They'll let us know if they extend the zone again."

Peter didn't want to remind them that most of the people killed in the 1980 eruption were outside the red zone, that authorities hadn't gotten it right back then. But the science of predicting eruptions had advanced a lot since then, Peter had been reading. Anyway, it'd be way cool to tell friends that he'd boarded down St. Helens right before it erupted.

They ate breakfast, pulled their gear together, and started hiking up Mount Adams. Jake and Mel in one pair, Peter and Susanna behind, Jarrad so far ahead that he was out of earshot.

"So, it's our last day on Adams," Peter said to Susanna.

"I know, and Jarrad said we could quit a little early to pack up camp. Maybe even stop and do some jibbin' at a BMX park in a town on the way to tonight's campsite. He said we could do that if we do really well today on the mountain."

"No kidding!" Peter said, astonished. He decided to ignore the "if we do well today," which sounded like a second-grade teacher's threat. A BMX park! That was great news because Peter ruled when it came to urban mountainboarding. That would open Jarrad's eyes to how valuable a guide he was.

"Yup. Maybe we can talk him into stopping for, like, ice cream, or even a movie!" Susanna said, beaming.

They'd come to a relatively flat area, and she was all but skipping like a kid, never mind the weight of her pack. It made Peter want to chuckle, all this newly unleashed energy in his girl.

"Whoa, don't get carried away, Suze. He's still Jarrad," Peter reminded her.

"We're not on this trip to spend time in towns," Mel spoke up impatiently ahead of them. "We're here to learn how to be better guides."

Peter stifled a smile as Susanna scrunched up her face at her sister. It was too much like someone making a face at themselves. He couldn't figure out why Mel wouldn't want cosmetic surgery on her face. She was so beautiful otherwise. But a serious and stubborn sort. Jake was welcome to her.

"We know this trail so well we shouldn't have to do it any more," Susanna said to Peter, in a petulant tone of voice. "Hey," she said, brightening. "Ever heard of Chinese Train?"

"Of course," Peter said. "Where a heap of boarders stays just behind each other following the same line and plays follow the leader?"

"Yeah, that'd be fun today," Susanna said.

"Right, you suggest it to Jarrad," Mel said flatly without turning around. Half sarcasm, half challenge, Peter decided. Why were these two being sassy to each other when they'd been so close and happy together before? Yeah, he kind of knew the answer. Mel had regained her confidence and skills, Susanna had been "released" from sister guard duty, and Susanna just wanted to have fun, which Mel probably disapproved of. Hey, Peter thought, Mel should be happy that Susanna didn't want one of the guide-job slots. Made for one less person she had to compete against. And anyway, since when was it a crime to want to have fun?

"I know what would be fun," Jake interjected, perhaps to ease tension between the twins, Peter thought. "Boarding with a kite. I've seen it done. Like having wings, or a sail."

"I've seen photos of that!" Susanna enthused.

"How cool would that be?"

"What's all the jabbering about?" Jarrad asked, having slowed to check on them. "No wonder you're moving like slugs in a drought. Put your dots in gear now!"

Peter accelerated his walking so fast that he heard Susanna complaining, "Peter, slow down!" But with Jarrad spinning around regularly to watch them now, he figured Susanna could do without him for a while. Time to take the lead, inspire the others, get up this mountain faster, he thought. Ten minutes later he noticed that Jake and Susanna had fallen well back, and Mel was only a footstep behind him, gaining on him with no sound of labored breathing. He quickened his pace even more.

"So, Mount St. Helens tonight," Melissa said, coming up alongside him. "Is it supposed to be easier or harder than what we've done already?"

"Way harder," Peter puffed.

"That's good. I like a challenge."

"Me too. Think the Convict will really let us get to a BMX park this afternoon?" Peter was only too aware that Mel was his main competitor.

"I don't see why not," she surprised him by answering. "Not for fun. To judge our freestyle skills."

"Is freestyle your thing?" Peter asked cautiously, trying to figure out how it could be if she was missing a hand.

She shrugged noncommittally, which made him uneasy. "I prefer downhilling." She slowed, a relief since he was getting winded. "Here we are."

And so they were.

"Okay, gang," Jarrad announced. "I'll be last today, watching for anyone incompetent enough to injure themselves. Go in whatever order you want. Last one down is likely out of the running."

Peter was on his board almost before Jarrad had completed the sentence. He deafened himself to Susanna's annoyed squeal, "Peter!" He felt, more than heard, Mel behind him. Besides Mel, he could care less where anyone else was, or whether they crashed and burned. He was going to clinch first place.

12 Freestyle

Jake sat on the park bench with two mountainboards either side of him, and one upside down on his lap. He was busy tightening Jarrad's egg shocks and axel nuts with tools from his tool kit.

He had no idea why he was here instead of in the ice cream shop with the rest of them. Jarrad had shot him a strange look when he'd volunteered to do tune-ups on the boards instead, as if Jarrad suspected Jake of trying to suck up to him after being last down the mountain today. He sure didn't know Jake very well if that's what he thought.

Jake adjusted the binding and turned the screwdriver so hard it almost beheaded the screw.

Peter had all but ignored Jake's jamming out, as if still sore that Jake wouldn't promise to "put in a good word" for him with Jarrad.

Jake let loose a bitter laugh. "Like Jarrad cares a

hoot what I do or say," he muttered to himself. "He hated my guts before he even met me, just because Nancy goes around telling everyone she likes me." He spun Jarrad's wheels to test them, then tugged at the bindings to make sure they were tight. "And even if he didn't hate me before, he does now, thanks to my blowing it almost every day." He pushed Jarrad's board off the bench onto the ground and pulled Mel's board gently into his lap.

And Mel? She'd looked a little disappointed, then squeezed his hand with a hint of sympathy in her eyes. Sympathy he really, really didn't need. She'd better not be thinking he'd "self-sabotaged" himself on today's run. He'd forgotten to check his tire pressure, that's all. And racked up some rotten road rash as a result. Maybe he'd skipped the ice cream session because he just didn't want to face her; maybe it was shame, humiliation. She'd finished second, barely a board's length behind Peter—way, way ahead of Susanna and Jake. Ha! She'd probably kept Peter hopping faster than a rabbit in Jarrad's gunsights, all the way down the mountain. Served Peter right for his over-the-top competitiveness.

Mel's board needed no tune-up he decided, after checking it over very carefully. She was obviously good at that herself. He stared at Susanna's well-used board as he reached for it.

Poor old Susanna. She'd looked too sore from the run, and too sore at Peter, to even notice Jake's exit. Peter's obvious campaign to get hired was pathetic. Jake was embarrassed for his buddy and starting to feel sorry for Susanna. She'd joined this trip on her parents' orders to look after Mel, and in hopes of having some fun as well. Neither mission was working out, and now Peter's focus on getting their boss to like him meant Susanna was starting to get bored and fed up with Peter. At least, that's what Jake thought.

He finished Peter's and Susanna's boards and set them down either side of him.

"Hey, Jake," Mel's soft voice came from behind him as he worked on his own board. An arm rested on his shoulder tentatively. "I brought you a mint chocolate-chip ice cream cone. Peter said that was your favorite."

He raised an arm to pull her around the bench beside him, then gave her a quick squeeze. "Thanks, Mel. Just needed some downtime."

"I know," she said, moving to sit on his other side—his right side—as if wanting to make sure he saw only the flawless half of her face. "You going to board in the BMX park?"

He shrugged uneasily. "It's not my thing, and I've had enough grief for today. Anyway, I want to check you out," he said, winking. He couldn't tell whether she was disappointed or not. But she squeezed his arm, teasingly pulled the tip of his baseball cap down over his face, and said, "Right then, I'm on it. With the best-tuned board in town, I presume."

"Hey, Jake. Thanks!" Jarrad said, appearing in front of the park bench a minute later and checking over Jake's job on his board. "You know your maintenance stuff, don't you?"

Peter drew up beside Jarrad.

Jake just about fainted to hear a compliment out of Jarrad. He managed an "Um, thanks" before noticing a shadow pass over Peter's face. What, Peter couldn't handle the Convict doling out compliments to anyone but Peter?

"Thanks, old buddy," Peter pronounced, picking his board up slowly and inspecting it like a paying customer. "No messin' with mine to make me look bad now, right?" He laughed as if it was the kind of joke they exchanged every day.

But it left Jake staring at him, speechless.

"Now there's gratefulness for you, huh?" Susanna said as Peter walked away. She plopped down on the bench beside him. The others entered the park half a block away. "You're not boarding in the BMX park?" she asked curiously, leaning down to collect her board. He caught the scent of peppermint and breathed it in like fresh air. He'd been telling himself all trip that he liked Mel, not Susanna, but they looked so much alike that he had moments where he was attracted to both, like he couldn't help it.

"Nope. Resting up for the St. Helens challenge," he said as lightly as he could. He watched the others inspecting the BMX park, but from where he sat, he couldn't see the park's features very well. He'd move to a bench nearer there in a minute.

"Hmmm. Would you mind, then, taking some pictures of me? And not all of me splatted on the ground, please," she added, giggling.

He blushed for no good reason, other than that she was overpoweringly good-looking, giggling at him, and leaning real close to show him how to work her camera. Maybe, too, it's because she looked so much like Mel that it was easy to feel way too comfortable around her.

"Of course," he said, his eyes on her locket—the one identical to Mel's—as it almost touched his forehead. "Susanna, can I ask what's in your locket?"

She looked surprised and straightened up. "Of course." She lifted the chain off her neck, popped it open, and held it up to him.

He found himself looking at a color photo of two Susannas smiling broadly at him. No, it had to be Susanna and Mel, before the fire. Before Mel's face had gotten messed up.

Susanna let him stare at it quietly for a minute. "I should get an updated one, I suppose," she said, voice wavering a little.

"You want to remember her like she was," Jake said so softly that he wasn't even sure he'd said it aloud. His eyes met Susanna's. He wasn't clear if he was telling or asking her.

Susanna snapped the locket shut and sat there, head hung low, flicking a finger against her mountainboard's wheels to spin them. "She shouldn't have gone back into the house," she said.

"But you saved her from getting hurt worse," Jake reminded her gently. "If it weren't for you …"

"I didn't save her!" Susanna said sharply, angrily, but seemingly to her mountainboard rather than to Jake. "My parents and everyone made out like I was a heroine. Kept saying how if I hadn't … Then they started depending on me to look after her while she was recovering … They still keep saying I'm the more responsible one. It's not true! It's not fair!"

To Jake's astonishment, tears started rolling down Susanna's cheeks. "They need to stop saying it. You need to stop saying it. I didn't do anything special. I grabbed her too late …"

She leaned into Jake, sobbing now. He felt obligated to put his arms around her. He understood, more than she would believe, this burden of being the favored one, the one considered so responsible. He understood how it could alienate others, even people close to you.

"Is that why you don't want to be a guide?" he asked her.

"Yes," she said between convulsions of weeping.

Without thinking, he began rocking her. "I understand, I understand," he was saying, stroking her hair.

"Susanna!" came a shout from the BMX park.

Jake and Susanna sat up rod straight, remembered where they were, and looked toward the shout. It was Mel, stump-hand on her hip, eyes flashing. "Are you coming, Susanna, or not?" she demanded loudly enough to carry to where they were. Peter stood not far from her, eyes narrowed at Jake, face cold. Jarrad was rolling down the gentle slope behind the park, crouching, going for big air.

Jake gulped for air of his own and leapt to his feet at the same time as Susanna. She walked away fast, board in one hand, other arm wiping tears from her face.

Jake slumped to the bench once she was gone, then took fully five minutes to stand up again and walk on numb feet toward a bench at the edge of the BMX park. Susanna's camera dangled in one hand, his board in the other, both feeling lifeless. He should snap a quick photo and then join them, show them he was competent at tricks. Not showy like Peter, but good enough. Show them he was part of the team. But he sat down heavily on the bench instead, feeling choked.

He raised the camera and aimed it at Mel, who was boarding so furiously that any image would be blurred. She took no notice of his lens's direction, just turned and sped away from him. As he swung the camera toward Susanna, he saw her beaming, posing, waving, obviously recovered from the emotion of their talk. She pumped down a ramp, lifted off, and twisted her body and board to the left. Then she snapped it back again and landed. Sweet, Jake thought as he saw the glow of satisfaction on her face. A Shifty Air. An easy but well-performed move. And a very photogenic model.

She turned and called out something to Peter, a big grin still on her face. But he turned his back on her and tromped up the hill. He kicked off like a racer and sped down toward the park. When he hit a ramp, he leapt aggressively into the air and squatted down to grab both the front and rear trucks of his board. He held them, held them—held them till Jake started anticipating him crashing like that—then released them and landed with ease. A Gorilla Air, Jake thought. An intermediate trick done with vehemence.

Jake turned back to Mel, pressing the camera against his face as if to hide the fact he was watching her. She came down the hill at a different angle, straight toward

of its binding and hold onto the binding to steady himself. He ended up returning his foot to the binding, grabbing the inside front foot with his front hand, and tucking in his knees, all in one swift move. A One-Footed Mute, Jake mused. Nicely done beginner's trick, even if he'd clearly meant to do something more difficult.

A loud "whack" made Jake swivel his head around. Oh-oh. Mel and Peter, riding down the track together, had got their wheels hooked up around a berm and crashed together.

As they tried to untangle themselves and their boards, they got even more entangled. They both stopped struggling for a second, lying there like a giant X: Mel's stomach on Peter's chest, board still on her feet and all askew, her head turned toward Peter's face. It made Jake uncomfortable, the way they lay there looking at each other, half-startled, half-amused. His body tensed watching them.

Finally, the two cracked up. Their laughter filled the air as Peter's arms came around her to pull her face closer. She seemed all too willing to let him. For a moment that lasted all too long, they looked like an item, like lovers. They made faces at each other, smirked close up. Peter's chuckles mingled with Mel's giggles until they were rocking with laughter together. Finally, Mel lifted herself off Peter, and he rolled over, detached his feet from his board, and stood. Still laughing uncontrollably, they put their boards aside and began play-fighting.

"You slid into me!" Peter was saying, trying to tickle her. "It's your fault we crashed."

"No," she said, squealing with laughter as she tried to tickle him back. "It's yours, you big bozo."

The scene was testing Jake's nerves mightily. Jarrad and Susanna stood watching them with mystified stares. Nothing was funny, Jake fumed. What was so funny? But the laughter continued pouring out of them.

Finally, as if out of breath, Mel rested her forehead on Peter's shoulder. Peter, still laughing, raised his arm and patted her on the back, drew her a little closer. Jake gritted his teeth and lowered his camera as Susanna shifted her eyes from Peter and Mel to Jake.

13 Total Eclipse

"I'm sleeping under the stars tonight," Susanna announced as Mel started setting up their tent at the Mount St. Helens campsite.

Peter didn't need to wonder why. The twins hadn't said a word to each other since the BMX park session earlier that afternoon. They'd sat far apart in the minibus, refusing to look the other's way.

Peter sighed. He should probably declare a desire to sleep under the stars, too—to be with Susanna. But he wasn't sure she wanted to stargaze with him. Plus, he was pretty ticked about her behavior at the BMX park. Embracing Jake in full view of everyone? Who'd started that? Hopefully they'd noticed the little act of revenge he and Mel had displayed to get them back. He was hurt and he was angry, and he didn't even know at whom.

"Mozzies'll eat you up," Jarrad said dryly, batting one on his bare, muscular arm.

"But there's supposed to be an eclipse tonight. A full lunar eclipse," Susanna said, tossing her mane of hair.

"Seriously?" Peter asked, not expecting that as her reason for moving outside. "That doesn't happen very often, hey?"

Susanna shrugged without turning to look at him. "Happens every few years or so. Only when the moon's full."

Peter looked up at the sky, vaguely impressed that she knew about such things. The sun was resting just above the western horizon, casting an orange-pink glow through tree branches in their campsite. A full moon was hanging in the sky to the east. A full moon. Fat chance he and Susanna were going to be cuddled together under it tonight, he thought bitterly.

Nor, for that matter, would Jake and Mel be, he guessed. Ever since Peter and Mel's "laugh-in" after tripping over each other at the BMX park, Jake had been avoiding Peter. But, hey, giving Mel a prolonged squeeze was just an innocent act of getting even. Fair's fair when someone seems to be stealing your girl. Peter kicked at the cold ashes of the campfire that a previous camper had left.

Anyway, Jake had been getting weird even before that. Withdrawn, sulking, not even trying. Was his buddy losing his nerve or just peeved that Jarrad didn't treat him the way Nancy did?

"I'm sleeping under the stars, too," Jake spoke up, interrupting Peter's train of thought. Jake pulled his sleeping bag out of the tent that he and Peter had just set up without once saying a word to each other.

Peter's throat swelled with panic: Did Jake have designs on watching the eclipse with Susanna? He stared first at Jake, then at Susanna, but neither was looking in his direction.

"Well, it's settled then. If the moon's doing a special demo tonight, let's all have a squiz at it," Jarrad spoke up cheerily, yanking his own sleeping bag out of his tent.

Peter wondered what the senior guide thought of all the tension in the air since this afternoon. Wondered if he'd noticed how or when it started. Wondered if he cared. Maybe his suggestion that they all watch the eclipse was his lame way of trying to cut through the strain without actually saying anything to anyone directly.

"That sounds like a good idea, Jarrad," Mel said, reaching into the tent after throwing a sour look at Jake.

Peter looked at Jarrad. The Aussie's hardened face was difficult to decipher, but Peter sensed a weariness, even a touch of bewilderment. Here was a guy who'd pitched them all against one another in the first place, and now he was trying to figure out how to deal with multiplying schisms between everyone? Peter had no sympathy for him. Peter was still set on winning the contest—to clinch one of the two junior-guide positions—but he didn't have a lot of respect for how the Convict was running things. Then again, Peter thought ruefully, Jarrad had doled out good advice at the start of the trip: "Sheilas: trouble, all of 'em. Steer clear if you have any sense."

Peter crawled into his tent to fetch one of his outdoor guidebooks. He sat down in a camp chair where he could watch everyone without seeming to, and flipped to the index to locate "moon."

By the time he'd turned to the page number listed, he realized he'd grabbed the wrong book. This one was on volcanoes. Then a sentence caught his eye.

"Hey, this says that full moons can help trigger volcanic eruptions. It says a full moon puts maximum stress on the magma—the hot liquid rock in the volcano's throat."

"Here goes Mr. Science again," the Convict mocked. "Are you trying to tell us that Helen is going to do a technicolor yawn while we're sitting on her?"

"What the heck is a technicolor yawn?" Mel piped up impatiently.

"It means to hurl, to vomit," Jarrad replied. He laid a big tarp on the ground and placed his sleeping bag on it, obviously planning to make good on his announcement that he was sleeping under the stars for the night.

"That's gross. Are all Australians gross?" Susanna asked. Whoa, even Susanna was getting impertinent to the head guide, Peter thought.

"Australians call it like it is," Jarrad retorted. "So, Mr. Science, I repeat: Are you saying Helen is going to blow any minute?"

"No one can predict when volcanoes will blow," Peter reminded them, "not even top volcano scientists. But there're always tremors before eruptions, you know. Maybe we should keep an eye on the wildlife around here. A few years ago in China, a mayor ordered everyone to leave his city based on how snakes and other animals were behaving. And sure enough, a few days later there was a major earthquake."

"Coincidence. Lucky guess," Jake said. "Sounds like folklore to me."

"Maybe," Peter said evenly. "But same thing happened before Mount St. Helens blew big in '80."

"Animals acted weird like how?" Mel asked, eyeing a squirrel scampering by the edge of their clearing.

"Birds go quiet. And snakes leave their nests, I read."

"Well, next time Jake runs over a snake," Jarrad inserted, "we'll have to decide if it was trying to slither away from an eruption or just aiming to trip him up." He laughed loudly as if covering up for the fact that no one else was chuckling.

"You're a jerk," Jake said, rising.

"I'm a what?" Jarrad demanded, twirling to face Jake.

"A jerk. You have no clue how to lead a trip. All you know is how to put people down and turn them against each other. How's that going to help us guide clients on a mountainboarding trip?"

"Watch your mouth, Golden Boy. And your attitude. Or have you forgotten you're here to keep your job?"

"I am a guide. And Sam and Nancy must've been out of their minds to hire you," Jake tossed back, leaning down in front of his tent to pick up a Frisbee. "Who wants to play Frisbee? We're supposed to be having some fun on this trip." Without waiting for an answer, he gave Jarrad a withering glare and strode away from camp.

Peter could hardly believe this. Was Jake nuts, talking to the boss like that?

"Frisbee?" Peter called out in disbelief after his buddy, making sure Jarrad heard and certain that Jake wasn't out of earshot yet. "What, you've got the energy for Frisbee, but you wouldn't even step onto the BMX park this afternoon? You claim you're a guide, but you were the last one down the mountain today? You've either lost it or you're a chicken, Jake. Go play Frisbee, then, if you don't have the guts to mountainboard any more."

Peter could hardly believe he'd said all that, but

he was fed up with Jake's strange, kamikaze behavior right from the start of this trip. It was almost as if Jake was messing up on purpose these days, or had given up. Peter wanted to shake Jake out of his funk, force him to turn and stand up for himself. Instead, Jake just kept on walking, Frisbee in hand.

"I'll play Frisbee," Susanna spoke up, an edge of defiance in her tone. "I say we all need to lighten up around here. And some of us need to stop sucking up to the Convict." She looked at Peter, then Mel, in turn.

"The what?" Jarrad shouted, his face contorted. He moved so fast he was a blur. Peter saw him clench Susanna's arm in his big hand. That rocketed Peter out of his seat and propelled him toward the two. But before he could reach them, Susanna had spun around and put her face right into Jarrad's.

"What, you hit Sheilas as part of training them?" she asked, holding his stare brazenly. She pulled her arm out of his loosening grip, turned her back on him, and walked off in the direction Jake had disappeared.

Whoa. Peter's throat constricted. Adrenalin was still pumping through him as he bent down to pick up firewood so Jarrad wouldn't realize he'd been about to fight him to defend his girl.

From that vantage point, he watched Jarrad's shoes shuffle over toward the picnic table, his hands reach down to pick up his clipboard, and his lower half wander a little uncertainly off in the opposite direction that Jake and Susanna had taken.

Silence hung heavily for a moment, till Peter turned to the site's only other occupant. "Right then. Well, Mel, guess we might as well get the campfire started." The words were barely out of his mouth when he remembered she was afraid of fire, still traumatized by it from her accident.

"S-s-sorry," he started to say, but she gave him a steely glare, kicked some wood from the woodpile toward him, and stomped off. The rest of the woodpile did a slow-mo avalanche onto his runners.

Oops. He sat down with his head in his hands. "Way to go, Peter," he mumbled aloud. "You're it, now. This is definitely not a group of happy campers."

He crouched on the ground and started picking up the firewood Mel had kicked toward him. Shadows lengthened around him, and cool air moved into the campsite. Frogs croaked in a disconcerting cacophony, announcing the fast-approaching nightfall. The grove smelled of pine and cedar. He shivered as he picked out the smallest bits of kindling and shaped them into a miniature tipi around some crumpled-up newspaper and dry pine needles in the center of the fire ring.

"They'll be back when they've all cooled off a bit," he told himself. "I'll get the marshmallows ready."

He got the fire started and rolled four big sitting logs into place at a safe distance from it. As the fire crackled soothingly and the throaty chorus of frogs seemed to settle down, he dragged his sleeping bag out of his tent and dropped it on the tarp Jarrad had set up. He lay down on it and looked up at the stars as they began to appear. He must've dozed off because he awoke with a start when Susanna spoke from her seat on a log near him.

"Here it goes."

He sat up, saw that the campfire was down to embers. Saw the silhouettes of Jake, Susanna, Mel, and Jarrad, each sitting on their own log around the fire. He looked up and saw the moon, unexpectedly bright white against the coal-black night sky. It was a white so luminous it seemed to pulse. And it wasn't hard to imagine a face in its little irregularities: a sad face, he felt. As he watched, a shadow crept slowly across the moon's face, like a dark hand moving to hide the sadness.

For an eerie second, it covered half the moon, making for a face half light, half dark. Peter glanced uneasily in Mel's direction, wondering what she was thinking. Then, more ominously, the sky went entirely black. All that remained in the silence was the pinprick of stars and a tinge of red—the color of dried blood—within the shadow that had devoured the moon. An unsettled feeling washed over Peter, something milder than panic. He suddenly understood why people used to be superstitious about eclipses, why some thought they predicted famine, disease, or a natural disaster. It no longer even sounded dumb that the Chinese navy still fired cannons to frighten the "dragon eating the moon."

But as surely as blackness had blotted out the white, the darkness moved slowly away, like a theater curtain signaling the next act of a play. Right before their eyes, the blackened moon renewed its white self and stared at them — unblinking, defiant, as if challenging them to read new superstitions into its bold metamorphosis.

14 Wipeout

Jake, awake with the sunrise, snuck out of his tent long before his snoring tent mate had stirred. He walked lightly through the dew-dampened grass, his prized compass in hand. Time to get lost and find myself again, he thought as twigs crackled underfoot. I'm up so early, he reflected in the still dawn, that the birds aren't even singing yet.

He fiddled with his compass bearings and headed to where his map indicated a viewpoint ridge. He stopped now and then to read his compass, sip from his water bottle, and pluck wild berries from bushes along the path.

Being alone and free was exhilarating. And he had no fear of a reprimand from Jarrad, who usually slept in even longer than the teenagers of whom he was in charge.

At least, Jarrad thought he was in charge of them.

The Convict thought he could command, divide, and destroy them bit by bit. But Jake had sensed a chink in the Convict's armor last night. Jake's and Susanna's open defiance and exit had thrown him off guard. He'd been mute the rest of the evening, just sitting there hunched on a log by the fire—no hat, no knife belt, no clipboard. There'd been a hint of defeat in the pale face lit by the full moon.

Jake didn't care. He didn't feel victorious, rebellious, or sorry for the man. Jake was on his own mission: to test his best orienteering skills. He looked up from his compass as a rabbit bounded off the path ahead of him.

The rabbit made him think of Mel. He had to patch things up with Mel. Last night, as he and Susanna had played Frisbee, he'd gotten her to promise to tell Mel that nothing was going on between him and Susanna. That embrace at the BMX park had just been an unlucky moment. He shouldn't have to apologize for comforting Susanna. He could totally understand Susanna's pain: her parents had pressured her into coming because they thought she was so responsible. Susanna shouldn't be burdened the rest of her life with the dubious title of heroine just because of a moment's impulse the night of the house fire. She shouldn't be "punished" with a job she hadn't asked for, to be her sister's guardian. She just wanted to have fun.

Jake was beginning to realize that he just wanted to have fun, too. Mountainboarding would be fun if it didn't come with Jarrad and a job-competition attached. Or clients and schedules and Nancy's notion that he was some kind of Sam's Adventure Tours hero, for that matter.

Last night, Susanna had told him why Peter was so fired up to snatch a guide position. Interesting that Peter hadn't shared with Jake the fact that his parents were so against his guiding, that if they had their way, this would be his last trip.

I want what Peter's got, Jake thought. I want the easy out he has: parents who have other options lined up for me. And Peter wants what he thinks I have: parents who approve of me guiding and a supposedly for-sure position within the company.

"But I want out!" Jake said aloud for the first time, startling himself. "I want to ditch this job."

Mel had suggested the possibility first. He'd been angry with her when she had. But now Mel was as caught up with getting the guide job as Peter was. Maybe Peter and I really should change partners, Jake thought ruefully.

He wondered what Jarrad would say if he told him he wasn't in the running for the job. He'd say good riddance, Jake thought with a snort. And what would Peter say if he told him he didn't want to work with

Sam's any more, that he wanted to go to summer school or travel or something? Probably wouldn't believe him.

He wondered what Mel would say if he finally admitted it. She wouldn't like me any more because she looks up to me as the model guide she wants to be, he thought uneasily. That decided it. He wasn't going to tell anyone. He'd just think on it a while, try and figure out what else he could do.

He looked down at his compass, only to see its needle shuddering. Jake blinked and drew it right up to his face. Still it shivered and convulsed. He shook it and looked again. This time, the needle pointed where he was pretty sure north was. At least, it had been north a few seconds ago. This is a brand new, expensive compass, he thought. It can't be packing up on me. Maybe I'm imagining things.

He swung toward where the viewpoint should be. Fifteen minutes later, he pulled up short. Whoa. The entire hike from the campsite, he'd been winding uphill through verdant, fresh-smelling green forests and ferns waving in the gentle breeze. But just across a gully from this viewpoint was the moon's surface. Well, it might as well be that: no trees, no animals, no snow—just highly unnatural sand-blasted rock. Like he'd lost his way and had ended up at the edge of the Sahara Desert.

Duh, he reminded himself. I'm on Mount St. Helens. It's amazing it's recovered as much as it has. What had Peter told him? In 1980, the volcano had belched up hot magma from its throat, throwing a plume of ash miles into the sky. Now there's a technicolor yawn for you, he mused, remembering the Aussie's expression. A blast almost a thousand times bigger than the atomic bomb that destroyed Hiroshima.

That herd of elk had been broiled instantly. Then rocks and ash had rained down on everything, and all the heat at the top of the mountain had melted its snow cone so that mudflows had moved down the mountain flanks, trapping alive anyone not already fried by the heat, pummeled by the rocks, poisoned by the clouds of gas, or choked by the ash. Yuck. And volcanic flows that no one could survive provided the finale.

But look now. Lots of it has healed, sprung back as if nothing ever happened. Except for areas like over there, which still looked pretty bleak. He craned his neck and tried to spot the summit high above him. Nope, no view of that. But he could imagine the steam puffing out of the crater, letting everyone know it was still an active volcano.

He checked his watch, realized he'd better hoof it back. He studied his compass readings. It's all good, he told himself. I can't get lost with this thing on me.

Even as part of him was tempted to let the compass

direct him down the mountain to someplace else—anyplace else—there was someone back at camp with a more powerful magnetic force field drawing him back. Mel.

As the sun rose over the treetops and he neared camp, he felt himself burning with resentment at Peter's last comment to him: "You've either lost it or you're a chicken, Jake. Go play Frisbee, then, if you don't have the guts to mountainboard any more."

Jake clenched his fists and tucked his compass into his pocket. I'll show him, he vowed. There's no yellow streak in me. I'll mountainboard him into the dust today. I'll make Jarrad's mouth hang open. I'll impress Mel.

* * *

"Jarrad, we're up and breakfast's ready," Jake heard Peter calling to the curled-up sleeping bag on the tarp.

The answer was a grunt. Then, "Go away."

The campers looked at one another, shrugged, and settled themselves around the picnic table as Jarrad resumed snoring.

"So," Peter said, holding up a book. "I've been looking at some stuff on volcanoes, and I want to read you what you're supposed to do if the mountain erupts while we're boarding." His grin prompted chuckles all him, like she was aiming to leap and land on him. Effortlessly, she lifted into the air and pressed her front left arm behind her front leg to grab her board's heel edge. At the same time, she let her front leg push the board down into a vertical position—"boned it." He clicked the shutter. She landed the trick. It was so tight that cheers erupted from her three fellow boarders. A perfect Meloncholliе Air, not an easy trick at all. But instead of looking elated over her success, Mel just grabbed her board and pressed her skater shoes onto the worn dirt path up the hill, her face hard. The shoes, he noticed, were starting to look worn now.

Jarrad had just climbed the highest point of the hill above the park. His board was still tucked under his arm. He was surveying the park's features like an army scout. Had his board been a spear, he'd have resembled an outback hunter moving in for the kill.

He lowered his board, clipped his feet into the bindings, and began a warm-up rocking. Jake challenged himself to capture the Convict in mid-air. Jarrad began rolling and pumping, picking up some real speed. He headed toward the biggest "table" in the park. Jake hoped he'd do a really tough trick, a 180 Switch Air, maybe, or a 360 Air.

But as he shot into the sky, his board wobbled a little. Others might have bailed, but Jarrad seemed to know he had enough air to shoot his front foot out around the group. Despite the tension from last night that remained thickly in the air, everyone seemed prepared to humor Peter this morning. Maybe their way of trying to get past that bad scene, Jake figured.

"Board like crazy, just ahead of the lava flow," Mel kidded.

"Nope. No fast lava flows here like in Hawaii. Helen is more explosive. She tosses masses of rocks and ash into the air. Most of the people killed in 1980 died of suffocation from breathing in ash. The rest died from rocks hitting their heads or mudflows catching up with them."

"So, whip out your iron umbrella and run while holding your breath?" Susanna piped up.

"That would be difficult, since the mountain erupted for nine hours during the big blow."

"Okay, so we out-board the rock showers and mudflows, and breathe through our T-shirts," Jake guessed.

"Half right, Jake. The books say not to run. They say stand still and look up at the sky so you can sidestep the biggest rocks coming down. You do that till the rockfall stops. Or till you get under an overhang."

"But you'd still be breathing in ash," Susanna pointed out.

"Right. For that, you're supposed to put on your gas mask."

"Gee, I think I forgot to pack mine this trip," Mel

said in a high-pitched, mocking voice.

"And if you don't have a gas mask," Peter continued, his finger on a line in his book, "you're supposed to pee on your T-shirt and breathe through that, because urine has something in it that counteracts the bad gasses, and the T-shirt will stop the ash getting into your lungs."

"Now that is just totally gross," Susanna declared. "You made that up."

"Did not," Peter said, handing her the book and pointing to the passage. She looked at it, then tossed it on the ground.

"Questions?" Peter asked, self-importantly.

"Oh, put a sock in it," Susanna said, standing up and walking over to Jarrad's snoring, as if trying to decide whether to kick him.

Jake picked up Peter's book to see how much Peter was making up. None, he was surprised to see. He was about to toss the book back down when a passage caught his eye: "Compasses are unreliable on active volcanoes due to magnetic forces ..."

He took his compass out, scratched his head, and read on, but all he could find was obvious stuff like, "Avoid river valleys, where poisonous gases, avalanches, and mudflows concentrate. It's impossible to outrun a mudflow, although cars have been known to outspeed them."

The sound of an approaching vehicle turned the youths' heads and caused Jarrad to stir. Jarrad sat up and rubbed his eyes as the car stopped and a skinny young man stepped out and nodded to him.

"Kids," Jarrad said a bit groggily. "This is Tommy, a local who's going to drive the minibus for us. I phoned and arranged it last night."

"Sweet!" Jake said. About time Jarrad arranged for a shuttle driver.

"All right!" Peter added. "No more trudging up for the rides down, and lots more time for mountainboarding."

"What's the latest news on St. Helens?" Jarrad asked Tommy.

"It's quieted down. Nothing happening. Just protests from logging companies wanting to reopen some of the restricted areas."

"Sounds good," Jarrad said, standing and stepping out of his bag to lope over to his tent for boarding clothes.

Two hours later, Tommy dropped them off at the trail's start, then drove away. "I'll lead," Jarrad ordered in a cranky voice. "Peter behind me, then the girls and Jake in that order."

Jake, determined to prove he wasn't the mountainboarding chicken that Peter had called him, ignored Jarrad and boarded into a position right behind the senior guide.

"What the deuces do you think you're doing?" Jarrad shouted at Jake. "You deaf?"

Jake lifted his chin and dared to meet Jarrad's fiery eyes with his fiercest show of defiance. "I'm boarding where I want to," Jake said.

Maybe Jarrad failed to see the gulp Jake had taken before saying that. Or maybe he was tired of fighting. Or he was saving himself for bigger fights. But to Jake's amazement, the big man just turned away and started boarding, with no further attempt to force Jake back into his assigned place.

Jake, both triumphant and uneasy at Jarrad's leaving things at that, boarded close on the guide's heels. He watched the big man's every move and tried to memorize every root and rock on the trail. He boarded so well that he fell only once the entire morning.

During the one break that Jarrad allowed, Jake plunked himself down beside Mel, who rewarded him with a warm smile and reached out her good hand to squeeze his. In contrast, Susanna and Peter sat apart, studying the ground in front of them. Oh well, Jake thought. That was their problem.

The second trip down, when Jarrad positioned himself at the rear to watch and critique everyone, Jake sped far ahead. Jarrad shouted at him, raged at him, but Jake ignored every word the Convict directed at him till he was out of earshot. Again, Jarrad seemed unwilling to take further measures to punish Jake for his defiance. And again, with a sense of victory dogged by surprise, Jake sped on ahead.

He bombed down sections so fast that when he met large rocks or sticks, he had only a split-second to pop into the air over them. A couple of times, he missed them by only a breath. But he continued boarding like a madman, and as his confidence grew, he felt as stoked about the sport as he'd ever been. In his mind, it was just him and the mountain, him and the sport, pure and wild fun, no one behind him.

He slowed on only two sections of the run. One, where the trail screamed around an elbow turn that nudged against a drop-off into a gulch. And two, where it dipped down into a gully beside a stream for a while before forking and offering the boarders a choice: a rise to a stony viewpoint or a tight left turn that hugged the stream for another ten minutes before rising and twisting back into the forest.

"Jake," Jarrad called out sharply during the third run, in a voice that sounded tired and half-hearted to Jake. "If you don't follow orders and if you keep acting like Speedy Gonzales, I'll have to—"

"You'll have to what?" Jake spoke up, chin raised high and his resolve strengthened by his success at defying his leader twice earlier. "Give me a speeding ticket?" That drew laughs from everyone, even Peter. And put a beautiful sparkle in Mel's eyes. The laughs silenced Jarrad, who couldn't seem to think of a comeback. He's starting to lose it, Jake reflected. His show of leadership is faltering.

More exhilarated than ever, Jake went for top speed the fourth journey down the trail. He knew it well now, knew every challenge it could throw at him. His teeth rattled against one another, and his legs sucked up the jarring ride like the shock absorbers on an expensive racing car. He was one with the mountain, a rocket on wheels, a plane accelerating to the speed of sound.

Coming up to the elbow turn—a particularly tight switchback—he remembered to crouch low and ride high on the edge of an upturned bank, ready to swivel his fully alert body at just the right second. But the right second never came because the trail edge on which he was riding collapsed with no warning, giving way. He fell hard maybe five feet down onto a dirt ledge only a few feet wide. Below him, where one foot dangled with his board still attached to it, the deep, dark gully he'd noted earlier threatened to swallow him. Fearful of ending up down there, he rolled back toward the wall to his left, only to be pelted by a new avalanche of gravel as someone else rode too near the edge. Instinctively, he pushed away from the wall just in time. A second later, a rider fell heavily beside him, pitching him over the precipice.

15 Busted

Jake knew the second his body hit soft dirt at the bottom of the gully that he was going to hurt head to toe the next morning. The wind was knocked out of him, and he could almost feel bruises rising. But he could move, which probably meant nothing was broken. He kicked his board off fast and scrabbled onto all fours to look up. A leg with a mountainboard attached to it was dangling over the precipice above, just as his had. That leg was attached to a body that was in severe danger of falling further. He recognized the boarding shorts on that leg.

"Mel!" he screamed. "Don't move!"

He looked about frantically, only to determine there was no easy way out of the gulch he'd dropped into. He stepped back to see if anyone—meaning Jarrad, Peter, or Susanna—was putting together a rescue from the road above. He was relieved when Susanna's head poked cautiously over the edge of the caved-in road. She was within arm's reach of her sister, he calculated; if she and Mel could join hands, she could stop her twin from falling down the second pitch. But it had to be fast, before Mel fell any further.

"Susanna!" he shouted at the top of his lungs. "Reach down and hold her hand! Quick!"

Susanna's eyes moved to take in Jake, but she didn't move. Didn't she realize how important it was to act immediately? She was plenty strong to just hold onto Mel's hand till Jarrad or Peter could help her. Hardly had that thought entered his mind when the memory of an order Jarrad had barked at Susanna half-panicked him: "Back off the poor thing. She's my job when we're on the trail!"

"Susanna!" he shouted again, as clumps of dirt fell down from beneath Mel's sprawled body. "Right now, right now! Just reach down and hold her hand!"

"Jarrad will help her," Susanna shouted back before withdrawing her head.

Jake watched Mel squirm just slightly, probably to roll a bit upward on the sloping ledge and back closer to the wall. But instead, gravity or her nervousness made her end up slipping even further from the wall. One move, one breath now, and she'd freefall into the gulch. And she might well not be as lucky as Jake.

He looked about frantically and began throwing

nearby cedar branches onto the ground where Mel would fall if she rolled off the precipice.

He saw Jarrad's and Peter's heads appear, and Jarrad extend his long arm to Mel. She raised her nearest arm, but the stump did not quite reach the guide's outstretched hand. She lowered it and started to raise her other hand, but that was all it took to undermine her balance. Along with a small avalanche of dirt, she fell onto the bed of cedar branches that Jake had barely begun to prepare.

"Mel," he said, bending over her. "Are you all right?"

She raised a hand to clutch her bleeding shoulder. She seemed too stunned to speak.

He extended his hand to help her up, but she brushed it away and slowly stood up by herself. "Just a scratch." She examined the gash on her shoulder, then brushed dirt off her body armor and looked him over. "You okay?"

"I'm good." He moved in close to embrace her, but she held one arm up to stop him and cupped the hand of her other arm protectively over her shoulder injury. "Don't touch it, please."

"Are you two okay?" Jarrad shouted from high above.

"We're fine," Jake shouted back, hoping it was true.

"Stand back. A rope's coming down," he announced. "It's anchored to a tree. Peter and I will pull you back up."

Mel accepted Jake's hand but seemed distracted either by her shoulder pain or the shock of the fall. "Don't help me up, okay?" she said as the rope end tumbled down.

"But," Jake objected, wondering how someone with just one hand could climb up a rope without help.

"I said stand back," she ordered in a tight voice as he leaned forward instinctively despite her request.

She wound the end of the rope around her right arm just above the stump, then placed the other hand above it. She pushed her boarding shoes against the dirt sides of the wall and waited to be dragged up.

When she was a few feet off the ground, Jake stepped forward to catch her if she fell. It's just as well he did; the rope slipped off her right arm and, despite an all-out effort, she couldn't hold on with just her left.

"No worries," Jake said as he held her in his arms, planted a quick kiss on her cheek, then eased her back to the ground. "Want me to help tie the rope around your waist?"

Her body was as stiff as her face. "Back off," she said, clenching her teeth and wrapping the rope around her right arm tighter. "I can do it myself. I've only just gotten Susanna off my back. Don't you start babysitting me."

Jake's chest went hollow, and he backed away

reluctantly. This time, she made it all the way to the top, her determined shoes finding holds on the dirt to help all the way up as the others above pulled.

When the rope returned, Jake tied his and Mel's boards to it, then watched them rise to the bank above. When the rope end dropped down again, he saved his rescuers a lot of effort by climbing hand-over-hand all the way to the top.

The five sweaty riders sat down heavily on the trail at the top. Mel, refusing Jarrad's help, busied herself wiping and bandaging her shoulder with supplies from his first-aid kit. Jake waited for the inevitable shouting and cussing from the big Aussie. But the Convict was strangely quiet, just staring at each of the teens in turn. Something about him was different, Jake sensed.

"Jake," he finally said in a deep but quiet voice, "you were boarding really well for the speed, but you overdid it trying to prove something, didn't you?"

Before Jake could respond, Jarrad turned to Susanna. "Susanna, when I told you to stop breathing down your sister's neck, I didn't mean to ignore your instincts. Kind of obvious back there you needed to help her right away, wasn't it?"

If the words sounded like Jarrad, the tone sure didn't, Jake thought. He wasn't shouting at anyone. His words didn't sound accusing or angry or manipulative. He sounded … well, like a coach discussing a game plan. Or a coach analyzing his players' strong and weak points. And he, the Convict, had actually used the word "instincts." As in, Susanna had ignored her own good instincts.

Jake watched Susanna's startled look before she hung her head to avoid Mel's eyes. Good instincts, Jake thought. That's what propelled Susanna to chase her sister the night of the house fire. Not some heavy heroic personality streak.

"Melissa, just 'cause you're way stronger and more gung-ho than most Sheilas with two hands doesn't mean there's some law against accepting help. Especially when a rock's taken a piece out of your shoulder."

Jake heard her take a deep breath, but she didn't reply.

"Peter, way to go, mate, helpin' me with the rescue." Peter mumbled thanks, looking from Jarrad to Jake as if stumped by the guide's change in personality.

Everyone watched warily as Jarrad stood now and dusted off his hands. He stared at each in turn—that intense, non-glaring stare. "So," he began, again in that calm coach voice. "Seems to me that if you four were actually trying to get along, none of this would've happened, yeah?"

The kids shifted uncomfortably.

"And maybe some of that's my fault."

He was met with four pairs of astonished eyes.

"But not all of it," he shouted, making them jump. He tucked the rope and first-aid supplies back into his pack and said, "Okay, you know the drill. Back on the trail, in whatever order you want."

In whatever order we want? Jake thought, wondering if he'd heard right.

"This is the last run down today." Jarrad stood back to let them go first.

One by one, they picked themselves up, helped themselves to drinks from their water bottles, and clamped their feet into their bindings. No one seemed willing to look at anyone. Shame hung over them like a black cloud. Busted, Jake thought. The Convict has actually figured out that everyone seems to have their own personal agenda. All the agendas clash. Well, he thought as he looked with a sigh toward Mel, so much for a united front.

He pulled his bindings as tight as they'd go and started down the mountain, well behind Peter and the twins. If Mel needed space, then he didn't feel like mountainboarding near her, or near anyone else, for that matter. He sensed that everyone else was feeling the same. Even Jarrad seemed to have given up trying to order them around. They spread out like never before.

Jake tried to tune into the surrounding forest to lower his anxiety, but it seemed to be harboring its own unease. Not even a trace of breeze stirred the branches, and the birds were taking a siesta or something. It occurred to him that he hadn't seen a living creature all morning.

He looked up as the trail emerged from the forest and cut across a rocky slope. The clear day offered a rare glimpse of the mountain's summit high above: white, glistening snow against an azure sky. He felt the view should comfort him, but it didn't.

He returned his attention to the trail as it headed steeply down. Back and forth it traversed now, demanding power slides so often that his calves began to burn. A stream trickled to one side, but he barely took notice of it. Back and forth, back and forth. Dizziness set in, dizziness so strong that it made the ground undulate like ocean waves. Rocks rolled randomly onto the trail, forcing him into a half-panicked slalom mode.

I'm hallucinating; maybe I'm suffering from heat stroke, he told himself as the dirt path beneath his wheels trembled and tossed. He felt himself pitched off the trail. He flew through the air so fast that he set off a sonic boom: A thunderous roar filled his ears before he landed and slid on his stomach the full length of his body.

Half deafened, he lay there clutching dirt in his gloves, even as the dirt shivered and shook. Jake rolled onto his back and looked up. His eyes bugged out of his head. A black, angry-looking mushroom-shaped cloud rose miles into the air overhead. Like someone had dropped an atomic bomb. Or maybe a bunch of them. Gone was the azure blue sky, and the mountain's sparkling white collar of snow was turning black before his eyes. Daylight itself was disappearing as he blinked.

He pulled himself to his feet and looked wildly about for his friends. A dust storm out of nowhere was blowing up, forcing him to raise cupped hands to his brows to look about. The stuff was as fine as chalk powder, and it worked its way into his nose and mouth even as he squinted almost to the point of shutting his eyes.

"Peter! Mel?" he shouted, then went into a coughing fit. His throat felt dry and irritated. He cursed himself for not staying within view and earshot of the others. *No way,* he suddenly realized. *Mount St. Helens has just blown. It really has. And I'm on it.*

"Jarrad! Susanna!" he screamed, but there was no reply. Just a rushing sort of sound, like a derailed freight train from high above coming at him. His face felt as if it was being rubbed by sandpaper. Above, lightning flashes fizzed and crackled between ominous dark clouds. The day grew darker and darker as he detached his board and scrambled to his feet. Then came the mother of all heat waves. As if someone had opened the door of a furnace and shoved him inside.

"Nooo!" he screamed as searing heat tore at his skin. His hands slapped at his arms as if he was on fire. He remembered the stream and stumbled toward it. He dropped onto all fours, then collapsed into the shallow flow, desperate for cool relief. "It's warm!" he cried in dismay. It was almost hot. Weirdly warm and gritty. And rising.

16 Heat

Peter tore his feet out of his bindings and staggered toward the stream, slapping at his exposed skin like it was crawling with biting fire ants. He screamed for his friends. He knelt right in the middle of the brook and bent down to splash his face—splash and splash like a crazy man. He drank some water, too, to ease a growing irritation in his throat.

He hadn't expected the water to be warm—warm as thermal hot springs—but it offered relief nonetheless. Enough relief to allow a terrifying thought to enter his mind. The shaking ground and mega-explosion could mean only one thing. Mount St. Helens, once again fooling all the experts who'd been monitoring her, had blown big.

"Jake!" he hollered in horror as he sprang up. He tore off a piece of T-shirt and held it low in front of him. He was shaking with such fright, he had no problem relieving himself onto it. Then, trying not to gag, he wrung it out and wrapped it around his nose and mouth like an outlaw about to rob a bank. It stank big time, was completely gross to breathe through, but he didn't care.

As fast as it had come, the heat wave subsided, as if someone had shut the furnace door. Peter pictured a wreath of super-heated air moving down from the mountaintop until it dispelled, like a ring of smoke from a cigar tip. Only fine ash falling from the sky offered proof that he hadn't imagined the whole thing. He hated to think how hot it must have been higher up on the volcano. If the mountainboarders had been at a higher elevation, they'd have been killed for sure, maybe even vaporized. He raced up the stream bank, his board hanging from one hand.

"Susanna!" he cried with relief as he saw Mel and Susanna kneeling at the side of the stream, frantically splashing each other. He charged over and, looking into their startled faces, said, "St. Helens! It erupted! Quick, pee on some clothing and wrap it around your face!"

Susanna stared at him as if he'd lost his mind.

"Protection from the ash, the gasses," he pleaded through his face covering. "Remember?"

Susanna hesitated, but Mel reached over to shake her sister's shoulder. "Susanna, he's right! Peter, turn away."

Peter turned around as Mel used her teeth to rip a strip from her T-shirt.

"Jake!" Peter shouted in relief as his buddy emerged from the heavy ash-fall a minute later. Jake was wet, covered in ash, and stumbling through the gloom like a zombie. He halted to stare at Peter.

"Peter! You're … What's that thing on your face? And theirs?" he asked, his eyes widening to take in the girls in their own cowgirl-style face bandannas.

"Those aren't … You didn't … "

"Think survival, Jake. Just do it!" Peter sighed with relief as Jake turned around and did what he needed to do before joining them.

The four embraced briefly, trembling.

"Where's Jarrad?" Peter demanded, his heart thumping as he turned upstream.

"Haven't seen him since before the explosion," Jake reported.

"Me, neither," each of the twins responded.

"We have to find him," Peter said, heading upstream along the ash-dusted trail. The others fell into line behind him, three dusty, sweaty gray figures in face masks, helmets, and body armor, toting their big boards. Even to Peter, whose mind was racing as quickly as his pulse, they made the strangest and smelliest medieval-looking procession ever to shuffle quietly through a forest in heavily falling ash.

"It's not getting darker," Peter noted loudly. "And the bad heat is gone." He meant the blast that had felt like the breath of a fire-breathing dragon. His face and unprotected portions of his arms and legs still stung as if seriously sunburned.

The four yelled for Jarrad till they heard a hacking cough from the darkened forest.

"Kids!" a voice finally boomed at them, relief in its tremor. A tall, ash-covered figure walked into sight. Peter winced to see Jarrad's face a mess of heat blisters. One gloved hand was over his mouth, uselessly trying to guard it from ash intake. The other clutched his board.

"Kids!" He sank to his knees, racked by more coughing. "I've been looking and looking for you ..."

They ran to him as if he was a long-lost father, not a despised boss.

Susanna raised her water bottle to his lips. Peter whipped off his bandana, tore it in two, and forced half of it onto Jarrad's face. "Jarrad, breathe though this. It'll stop your coughing."

Jarrad gasped and gulped and stared at them. Then he tore off the urine-soaked mask and stood up, wavering as he held the cloth pinched between gloved fingers. "Crikey! Who shoved this on my face? This is no time for jokes!"

"Jarrad," Peter said. He got as far as explaining the mask when Jarrad cut him off.

"No time to talk, kids. We gotta get down to

camp, then drive out in the van. Don't be scared. Just follow me!"

He clicked himself into his bindings and began boarding down the trail, his wheels creating tracks in what looked like a thin layer of snow. This was where the trail headed down to run alongside a stream, in the bottom of a gully.

Peter hesitated, trying to decide why it didn't feel right, but as the other riders stepped onto their boards and took off after their leader, he followed. As they followed the trail down, down, and down, it was slowly disappearing under ash. At least the stream just to the right of it helped identify where they were, Peter thought. Soon, a bank rose to their left, and another to the right of the stream bed. The group had ridden this section on their previous trips down, but never before had Peter felt so constricted by the deepening gully. High above, the walls even bowed in, as if trying to form a giant half-pipe or roofless tunnel.

"How far's camp from here?" Susanna asked Peter in a nervous voice as she drew up beside him.

"Not too far," Peter muttered, wishing he could be more reassuring. He saw Susanna shudder, then realized the ground beneath them was shuddering. He jumped as a deafening explosion ripped through the mountain yet again.

"No!" Peter screeched as tiny rocks fell from the

sky and pinged off their helmets. He turned his eyes upward to see the dust storm turn to hot hail. Glancing backwards, he was just in time to see two giant, scorched tree trunks roll down the embankment and wedge themselves side by side into a thick, angular arch over the trail.

"Faster! Gotta make it to camp!" Jarrad was shouting, jabbing a gloved finger wildly downstream. With his other hand, he fished his clipboard out of his pack and held it up like a visor to keep rocks from hitting his face.

"No!" Peter screeched louder. "Back there, under the logs!"

The others went into power slides on the slippery ash and turned to stare first at Peter, then at Jarrad, as the hot rockfall picked up. Confusion and terror flooded their eyes.

Jake was the first to jump off his board and sprint back up the trail toward the rough lean-to that the fallen tree trunks had formed. The girls hesitated only a second before following.

That left Jarrad standing alone, waving like a crazed creature under his clipboard. "Downhill to camp!" he insisted angrily, but no one was listening.

A chip of falling pumice stung Peter on the back of his neck before it hit the ground, glowing as red as a hot coal. Another branded one of his wrists. He risked a glance skyward as larger pebbles hit his armor like slingshot stones. "Walk! Don't run!" he ordered. "And look up, like this!" He raised his eyes again just in time to dodge a deadly, baseball-sized chunk of magma.

He remembered reading about a soldier in a tiny guard-post hut near the rim of a volcano called Galeras in Colombia. When rocks had started coming down during an eruption, he'd stuck one hand with upturned palm out the door like someone might do to feel the first drops of rain. A falling rock had instantly shorn off his hand. But he'd lived.

As the girls and Jake slowed and stared at him, Peter continued to shuffle toward the logs, face exposed upwards to the barrage so he could sidestep any chunks that looked capable of crushing his skull, helmet and all. He ignored the searing pain of smaller rocks burning him anywhere his body armor didn't protect him. It was a price he needed to pay to stay alive. He looked up, took a step, looked up, took a step—side-stepping like a skittering lobster toward the fallen tree trunks. He dove into the lean-to just ahead of Jake, breathed a shaky sigh of relief, and gestured to the others.

"Keep coming. That's right! And keep looking up!" They were moving like a dance troupe doing a weird routine. All except Jarrad, who stood there wailing, "To the van, to the van!"

"Jarrad, look up!" Peter shouted as a sharp-edged rock hit Jarrad's clipboard and broke it in two.

Jarrad lowered the two halves of the burned clipboard and stared at them. He let the pieces drop to the ground and began sprinting wide-eyed toward the group now huddled under the logs.

"No, walk!" Peter and Jake yelled in chorus, but it was too late. A soccer-ball-sized piece of hot pumice cut the giant down. He fell heavily face-first to the ground, sending up a small cloud of ash.

Peter and Jake shot out of the shelter. They grabbed their stunned leader under his armpits and, still looking up at intervals, pulled him the remaining distance to safety without being hit hard themselves. He groaned and momentarily opened his eyes as everyone kneeled around him.

"He's breathing," Jake reported after checking Jarrad's pulse and lowering his ear over the man's mouth. Jake pointed to a dent in Jarrad's helmet and a large black burn on his armor between his shoulder blades. The fabric was seared as if a hot iron had sat on it for too long.

"His helmet and armor saved him," Jake said shakily. "Jarrad, Jarrad, are you okay?"

"The van, back to camp," Jarrad muttered in response, eyes opening and closing again as Jake and Peter examined him from head to foot.

"He's okay, maybe just disoriented. Face is really burned," Peter ruled, listening to the rain of rocks on their roof.

"Lift his legs so he doesn't go into shock," Jake reminded Peter.

"And loosen up tight clothing," Peter said, reminded of the second rule for trying to prevent shock. He unbuckled the belt holding Jarrad's knife sheath, and adjusted it.

"How long is this going to last?" Melissa spoke up, shivering in the heat as the boys lifted Jarrad's legs.

"Who knows?" Peter replied, moving to embrace a trembling Susanna. "But we must be on the edge of the blast, not wherever the worst of it was, or we'd be done for by now."

"Done for?" Susanna asked tremulously, slipping her gloved hand into his.

"Poisonous gases," Peter replied. He flinched as a thud on the logs overhead vibrated the entire structure. For a fleeting second, he felt like he was in a war zone, huddled in a bomb shelter targeted by ballistic missiles.

It was Jarrad, still lying on his back, who broke the next stretch of silence. "Roof's on fire," he stated so calmly that Peter figured he really was going into shock.

Next thing Peter knew, Jake had sprung up and just out of the shelter. He was visible only to his chest as he raised his arms to heave something off the roof. Then he yelped, dropped back down, and rolled in. He was staring at his gloves, whose fingers were burned right off, exposing pink, raw, charred fingertips.

"Don't … touch … the rock up there," he mumbled with a grimace as his injured hands moved to his armpits. He'd hardly finished speaking when Melissa rose and pushed her head out of the shelter.

"No, Melissa!" Peter shouted at the same time as Jake. But as the two boys lunged to pull Mel back in, Susanna rose unexpectedly with raised elbows to block them both.

"Let her!" Susanna screamed as Mel flung her upper body at the basketball-sized piece of pumice on the roof.

The huge rock, glowing an eerie red-orange, dropped off the shelter, glancing a blow to Susanna's helmet on its way to the ground. Mel, ignoring the smoke coming from the remnants of her stump's glove, gave the glowing rock a swift kick, burning a hole in her right shoe as she did so.

Susanna crumpled to the floor of the shelter and covered her face as if fighting tears. Mel grabbed water bottles and spilled their contents onto the roof, which sizzled in response.

Only as Mel squatted down, tripping over Jarrad's legs, did Peter realize what she had just done: she'd overruled her fear of fire and used her already-burned stump to push the rock off the roof with adrenalin-fueled super-strength. Susanna had somehow anticipated her twin's intentions and allowed Mel to do it.

Perhaps Mel could have, or should have, used something else to move the rock. But she and Susanna had known they had to act quickly to save them all. They'd responded before the log shelter could burst into flames, and before the boys or a half-conscious Jarrad had fully appreciated the danger or formed a plan.

Peter reached for the first-aid kit attached to Jarrad's waist belt, unzipped it, and spilled out tubes of antiseptic cream and bandages. He gazed from a sobbing Susanna to Jake's burned gloves, to Mel's blackened stump and Jarrad's pale face.

"Stay calm," he told himself. He heard Nancy's voice in his head: "Never let favoritism for friends get in the way of a professional assessment in triage."

"Susanna's okay," Jake reported, "just scared."

"And Jake's and my burns will heal," Mel was saying. Peter nodded soberly as he turned to Jarrad. He raised the man's legs again and pulled some clothing from his backpack to pile onto the man. That was the other way to try to stop someone from going into shock, Nancy had taught them.

He looked at Mel's and Jake's blackened wounds next. His memory flashed a picture of last night's lunar eclipse: from white to black to white again.

Yes, the burns would mend. He realized that the very ground on which they were sitting had been scorched by eruptions and renewed itself numerous times. Mel was right. She knew better than any of them what could heal.

Gently, Jake helped Peter apply ointment to Jarrad's facial burns as the man blinked passively. Peter then extended burn treatments to Mel, then Jake, before taking a calmed-down and grateful Susanna into his arms. Eventually, he treated his own, more minor burns.

"We all have burns, but we're all alive," he said. He looked outside the shelter. "And the rockfall's easing up."

Indeed, it stopped as suddenly as it had started. That made Peter swivel his head to look at the stream. He drew in his breath. Instead of water—even steaming water—the creek was now oozing heavy and grey, like someone had upset a giant bucket of liquid concrete upstream.

"Stream's rising," he warned. High up the mountain above them, white glacial snow and black hot ashes were clearly combining to form a sludge running down the mountain. Like ice cream melting in slow motion, it was flowing wherever gravity took it. Perspiration ran down Peter's face. Why hadn't he foreseen it? Their trail ran alongside a stream. The stream and trail together fit into a gully that, where they sat right now, featured impossibly steep sides. If the mud-engorged stream rose to swallow the trail, it would be difficult to claw their way up to safety before the mud swallowed them alive. Twenty-seven bodies were never found after the 1980 eruption, he remembered.

"We have to get out of here," Jake pronounced before the words were out of Peter's mouth. "We have to get to where we can climb out of this ravine."

17 Mud

"No," Jarrad shocked them by barking out as he grabbed onto a piece of Jake's T-shirt with both hands. "We stay here. Don't you kids get out of my sight again."

Jake pried off one of Jarrad's hands and recalled a place where the trail forked not far ahead, the left side leading up and out of the ravine, the right side continuing beside the stream on the right. That fork wasn't far ahead. It couldn't be far ahead.

Melissa's trembling finger pointed at the stream bed's ooze as it carried by the carcass of a fox. "Maybe it won't rise to our shelter."

"It will," Peter predicted solemnly. "Jake's right. We have to move."

"Now!" Jake added, scrambling to his knees. Even as he shoved everyone's mountainboards at them, Jake's mind recalled a schoolbook photo of a man dying in agony in Pompeii, Italy—a man whose terror-struck facial expression and outstretched hands had been perfectly preserved by layers and layers of compacted ash for two thousand years.

"No!" came the final objection of someone whose very authority, and grip on Jake's shirt, seemed to be dying.

"Jarrad, can you board?" Jake demanded fearfully. What would they do if he couldn't?

Jarrad's eyes flickered from murky to alert, and the man's hand rose to rub his face where Jake had applied some antiseptic cream. "Of course I can board," Jarrad replied indignantly. He struggled to sit up, then lurched to his feet. He shoved his feet into his bindings and tightened them with three practiced tugs. He might be operating on autopilot, Jake reflected, but the seasoned boarder's instincts just might get him to safety.

Five frightened survivors emerged from the shelter and pointed their boards down the trail as the rising stream of mud nudged toward it. Jake took a deep breath to try and steady his nerves. The muggy air smelled of sulfur and ashes. Larger and larger tree branches, plus occasional animal remains, were powering down the mudflow beside them. Not a bird or insect was in sight. Every carve the riders made around rocks in the trail sent up plumes of ash—like mountainboarding on the moon, Jake reflected. Grass along the trail had been burned so badly that it crumbled to dust as the group rode over it. Ash covered everything like a toxic snowfall.

It had been as dark as evening ever since the first eruption, but enough sun filtered through the ash-choked sky to light the boarders' way as gravity granted them speed.

The mudflow roiled and rose, steamed and swelled, lapped and swallowed, ever more crazed by its own volume. Jake led, looking—ever looking—for the fork that would allow them to board up to that scenic point, the fork that could take them out of this half-pipe-shaped chasm, this narrow valley of death.

"So we headed down this pipe on our boards. Figured it'd be an easy ride, that we'd get to work up some speed, maybe hit thirty miles an hour. Didn't reckon on some idiot who didn't know we were there opening the sluice gate and letting water out when we were about halfway down ..."

Jake looked back to see Peter boarding beside Jarrad, reaching out to steady or encourage the spaced-out guide when needed. Jake wondered if Jarrad had suffered a concussion. So far, the Aussie's instincts were serving him well. The twins brought up the rear.

Even as the muddy maelstrom began inching onto

their trail, Jake was relieved to find fewer and fewer obstacles in their path. They were now beyond where most of the mountain's molten rocks had fallen, and he was certain the fork he was seeking was around another bend or two.

Jake sped up with growing confidence. For the first time, he was thankful Jarrad had pushed them as hard as he had over the past week, emphasizing both technique and speed. He'd taught them to leap objects instinctively. Jake was also thankful that everyone knew the trail so well—even if it seemed far more than a few hours since they'd launched on this, their fourth run down the mountain.

The thwack-thwack of helicopter blades sounded high above—too high, Jake feared, for anyone to spot the mountainboarders.

"Jake!" Peter's shout from behind interrupted his thoughts. He turned to see Peter, wide-eyed, gesturing behind them, upstream. Jake's heart all but stopped. A wall of water—no, make that thick mud—was coming down the gully like a slow-motion rogue surf wave. Coming at them at maybe twenty miles per hour. Big Foot had nothing on this terrifying sight.

"Board for your lives!" Jake screamed as he saw Jarrad halt and stare, Mel and Susanna sprint forward at high speed, and Peter tug at Jarrad. Jake spun and powered down the trail faster than he'd ever boarded in his life.

"It's impossible to outrun a mudflow!" Peter shouted at Jake, his voice on the edge of panic.

"But not impossible to out-board one," Jake shouted back as the fork he'd been waiting for came into view. He made a quick calculation: Safer to keep hurtling forward until the left turn's uphill forced him to leap off his board and run, than to jump off the board now and attempt to scrabble up the steep bank beside them.

He could hear the low growl of the mud tsunami, the rearing mud wave. Could all but feel its hot breath on his neck. He locked his eyes on where the trail split and sped toward it like a trucker without brakes might dash for a mountain runaway lane.

Time to break all mountainboard speed records. Four other lives depend on me getting to safety, he realized.

"Go, go, go, go!" came Jarrad's booming voice well behind them. Whatever brain-shaking the Convict had suffered sure hadn't affected his lung power, Jake decided.

Jake boarded faster, faster, and still faster, till all but the trail in front of him became a blur. He let his knees suck up the jarring ride, kept his arms stabbing out for balance like a crazed orchestra director. If his board had been outfitted with a speedometer, he guessed it'd be hitting more than sixty miles per hour right now. As long as they were speeding faster than that mud wave behind them, they were all right.

Two minutes, three minutes—he lost all sense of time in the chase. He dared look back only once to make sure everyone was still there and on their boards. The nasty mud-curler was still in sight, even if slightly farther behind them than before.

He jabbed his left arm toward the left fork to alert his followers, and bent low to take the rough transition. At teeth-chattering speed, he wobbled and nearly fell as the board tore uphill. With careful timing, he leaned back to help lift the front of his board. That kept it climbing as high as it could before it lost momentum. Suddenly, he snapped it ninety degrees to try to stay perched perpendicularly on the track and prevent the board from backsliding very far.

As he slid to an abrupt stop, he fell face first onto the ground, where he hugged the gravelly trail as if it was a crucial handhold on a vertical cliff wall. He didn't mind at all when first Mel, then Susanna fell on top of him. Soon it was one big dog pile of boarders. Everyone was trying to scramble higher while looking with horror at the oncoming mud rush.

Jake heard a guttural, gurgling sound and felt warm mud spatter him from head to toe. Shrieks from the mouths of his fellow boarders, and the sharp pinch of arms trying to hold onto his waist, made him grip the ground harder.

"Jake!" he heard someone wail in a voice that trailed off eerily.

He raised his head, rolled out from under the heap, and untangled his limbs from those of the twins. Then he stared, horrified, at what had turned from a sleepy stream to a canyon nearly full to the brim with sludge. The brown mess churned with enormous stumps and charred trees. Straddled on one of the logs, which was fast disappearing around the bend, was a mud ghost. No, make that Peter, ghoulishly draped in the thick goo, one arm trailing in the current to hold onto a floating helmet. The helmet, he realized just before both disappeared from sight, held Jarrad's mud-covered head, which appeared to be struggling to stay above the surface. Just seconds before, Jake was sure, all five had formed a human chain of boarders pressing their bodies to the trail.

"Peter!" came a despairing cry from Susanna beside him as she leapt up. "Jarrad!"

Jake shot to his feet, pushed ahead of Susanna, and began sprinting along the upper trail, trying to regain sight of the river victims. But the current was flowing faster than he could run, and one false move meant he'd slip and plunge down the bank into the mud's grip. Maybe he should just jump in? No. He'd only become a third victim.

He ran and ran, his heart pumping so wildly he could barely hear the ugly sounds of the flooded river and the banging, bumping, and grinding of the trees it was dragging along.

"Nooo!" he screamed as the trail came to a dead end, all but slamming his face into a cliff wall. It rose to impossible heights above and without a handhold to be seen. Jake leaned precariously out over the river, still searching it, but Jarrad and Peter had long disappeared ahead. Susanna and Mel must've thought he was leaning too far out because they took hold of his elbows and dragged him back, forcing him to sit on the trail where it ended.

"Nothing more we can do, but they'll make it to shore," Jake said with a choked voice. But silently, his brain was shouting, "I failed again. I didn't board fast enough."

He pressed his face into his hands.

"Camp's not far away," Mel said in a flat, dull tone.

"Camp," Jake said gently, "is buried under tons of mud by now." The minibus, he realized, would be just another object bobbing in the monster-river's grip.

The twins shivered, prompting Jake to shed his pack and search it for the emergency space-blanket it held. He wrapped the crinkly fabric around the three of them like a shawl.

Mel leaned into him. Susanna kept staring downstream, mute. Susanna, Jake reflected with irony, had joined this trip just to have fun. Less than half an hour ago, it had been she who'd allowed Mel to stop their little log shelter from burning. That had been brave; she'd acted on what Jarrad had dubbed her good instincts. Now, all too soon, she was grieving for Peter, whose only fear on this trip had been that it might be his last as a junior guide.

"Peter will be okay," Jake said softly, squeezing Susanna's shoulder. "His instincts are as good as yours." She looked at Jake tearfully and didn't argue with his compliment.

Jake was not certain, however, whether Peter could rescue Jarrad. Jarrad, Jake reminded himself, had been asleep when Peter had advised everyone how to react to an eruption. Plus Jarrad, although strong and fit, was suffering from a possible concussion because he'd placed no value on Peter's book knowledge. Jarrad, so focused on whittling four junior guides down to two, was now fighting for his life, his fate in the hands of just one.

How long Jake and the twins sat huddled in the false twilight, as ash continued to drift down on them, Jake had no idea. He came alert again only when the thwack-thwack of a helicopter sounded overhead. He fought to stay awake now so he'd be ready to wave if the helicopter came near. And if it didn't? It would be a chilly night, but they had each other and the space blanket. They'd come through the worst already. They'd survive.

18 Log Ride

One second Peter had had his arms around Susanna's waist on the steep trail and was yelling, "Hold onto me, Jarrad!"

The next second, an overpowering slap of mud had sucked him and Jarrad away from their companions—as if the river required two bodies in exchange for letting three go free.

Pulled completely under in the warm, moving guck, Peter flailed and fought, unable to determine up from down as the current and its debris smashed and pummeled him. Rubble pierced and tore his body armor, bruising and cutting him.

Just as he thought his lungs would burst, a big hand grabbed him under an armpit and lifted him to the surface like an iron hook. It was Jarrad. It could only be Jarrad, Peter thought with overwhelming relief and gratitude.

"There!" Jarrad gasped as he shoved Peter up onto a log floating beside them. Peter slid along his chest and stomach—rough, blackened bark biting into the gashes he'd acquired underwater.

Somehow, before Jarrad could let go of him, Peter managed to reach around and clutch Jarrad's helmeted head, which he held onto like a prized bowling ball. No way was he going to let them get separated now.

The air still felt thick with ash, and Peter's eyes hurt when he rubbed them. *Must've collected grit when I tried opening them underwater,* he reflected. Blinking to ease the discomfort, he took a quick look around.

Dead fish, carcasses of unidentifiable, mud-covered animals, and logs of every shape and size jostled for space in the roiling river current. Above, trees felled by the blast had spilled down the riverbanks like toothpicks, blocking any attempt Jake might have made to help rescue Peter and Jarrad.

Jake and the twins are okay. They'll be rescued, Peter assured himself.

The river wasn't wide, and had he been alone, Peter might have considered jumping from one log to another to reach shore. But his only thought now was pulling Jarrad up before debris slammed into their log and crushed the man to death.

"Jarrad," Peter shouted above the slurping noises of the charging mudflow, "Can you swing a leg up here?"

Jarrad's mud-encrusted eyelids flickered open, but he only shook his head. Defeat hung in his eyes before the lids shut again. His handhold loosened on the log.

"Jarrad!" Peter pleaded, terrified at the thought that the guide might have spent the last of his energy boosting Peter onto the log. "I'll haul you up somehow. Just try and help!"

With one hand still clamped on Jarrad's helmet, Peter rose and wriggled around to ride the log horse-style, hoping that would buy him enough leverage to pull on Jarrad. But hardly had his left ankle touched the mudflow when a log rammed theirs from behind, all but toppling Peter off. He decided against exposing his lower legs to where they could be shorn off by passing debris.

A noise from the sky made him look apprehensively upwards. What he really didn't need now was a new eruption. But as the noise grew louder, he recognized the rhythmic beat of helicopter blades.

"Yes! Here! Here!" he screamed, waving one hand wildly while the other clung to Jarrad. "We're going to be rescued, Jarrad. Wave if you can!"

But just as quickly as it had appeared, the big bird carried on downstream, oblivious to the two mud-drenched humans in the muddy river torrent. Peter's jaw slacked open. "How could they not see us?"

he cried in disbelief and bitterness. "Jarrad! They missed us!"

There was no response from the man still immersed in the river. Peter wondered how long he could keep a handhold on Jarrad. His arms were feeling stretched to their limit. The muggy, smelly air and eerie heat of the roiling mud around them was making him sweat buckets and yet shiver at the same time.

"Can you lift your arms?" Peter begged, certain that if he let go, the man would sink out of sight forever. Kneeling on the log this time, he placed his hands under the guide's arms and attempted to lift him. He couldn't believe the strain this effort required. Like trying to pull someone out of tar.

Still, he managed at last to position both of Jarrad's hands on top of the log and the man's forehead against the log's right side. After a breather, he applied everything he had. He strained, he shouted, he twisted, but how could a kneeling boy pull the dead weight of a full-grown, half-conscious man aboard a moving vessel, even if the man had been suspended in water instead of flowing mud?

Sweat poured down Peter's face, and desperation set in. I can't do it by myself, he realized.

"Jarrad! Jarrad!" He forced the man's eyelids open with a thumb, which elicited a grunt. He's conscious, but only barely, Peter realized. He kneeled on Jarrad's hands to hold them on the log and looked warily about, still panting from his efforts.

Logs knocked against each other, sometimes noisily shearing bark one from another. Ahead, Peter saw the roof of a car sinking slowly between two trees. Had someone been in it, or had its owner gotten away? Barely in view ahead, he caught sight of a bridge span. Behind him, he spotted the remains of a tattered red tent half caught on the roots of a bobbing stump. He stared at this small patch of color moving slowly through a world of mud and ash. He was sobered by the notion of innocent outdoor campers caught along the scenic shore of the Toutle by this unfathomable nightmare.

For another second, he turned his head back and forth between the muddy red tent and the upcoming bridge span. New energy stirred as he formed a plan.

His eyes squinted at the tangled assortment of roots on a stump headed toward them. In the second it took for the stump to pass, he leaned out precariously, one leg still clamped on Jarrad's hands.

He leaned further, hands reaching, grasping. Just a little more, he told himself, heart thumping wildly. Finally he had a fistful of roots in one hand, and one edge of that bright piece of mud-splashed red tent. He was now in a tug-of-war for the tent and the stump around which it was wound. His body bridged and stretched between his log and the stump like a medieval torture rack that stretched people till they burst into halves. He gritted his teeth. It would take every muscle he had to bring the two together. Failure meant he'd flop in and Jarrad would probably sink, both of them left to the whims of this writhing, debris-clogged river.

Slowly the stump drew toward Peter's log, and his log drew toward the stump. Slowly, he forced them alongside one another, steering the log a little closer to shore. At last, with the torn, muddy red tent triumphantly in his hands, he began to rip and tear half of it into shreds.

He used the first strip to tie the log and stump together. That stabilized and slowed the log. Now we're like a canoe with a pontoon on one side, Peter decided, one eye on the approaching bridge span.

The next strip he quickly wound around Jarrad's chest and the log, to hold him to it. Now, working even faster, Peter plunged his head into the muddy river to wind a third strip of tent fabric around Jarrad's groin and leg. Gasping and shaking his muddy head like a wet dog, Peter then pulled and pulled on that underwater lasso to bring first one, then the other of Jarrad's legs up to the log. Only seconds later, a log rushed at where the man had been hanging and banged it hard, as if furious to have missed crushing a victim.

"Almost there, Jarrad," Peter said through gritted teeth, gently massaging his knuckles into the guide's muddy face in hopes of a response. "Stay awake, Jarrad, please. You have to try to stay awake!"

"Mmmm" was all that came from the Aussie's mouth, but that was good enough for Peter.

He plunged his hand into the river, grabbing a floating stick to use as a pole, then leapt from log to stump to log again, steering, spearing, prodding, poking, and pushing his strange-looking vessel between other logs to shore.

"Yes!" he shouted in victory as the log-stump raft touched land and spun drunkenly for a second.

Hurriedly, Peter laid what remained of the red tent on shore, released Jarrad, and gingerly pulled him onto the tent. Then he pulled the muddy fabric, like a picnic blanket transporting a sleeping picnicker, up the hill to the abandoned road that crossed the bridge span.

The bridge itself was unusable, the middle section of it having fallen into the current. Peter cringed as he pictured someone downstream being hit from behind by that missing piece of steel bridge span instead of by a mere log.

"They'll see us here," he told Jarrad, rolling thc man off the tent, then wiping swaths of mud from it so it turned red again. "The rescue helicopters will see us, I promise."

He climbed the upper supports of the broken bridge span and hung and tied the red tent across them as best he could. The one corner he couldn't secure began flapping in the breeze. That's not a bad thing, he decided, climbing down again to examine a sleeping Jarrad, who was shivering.

Jarrad, still soaking wet, was trembling, almost convulsing. All Peter could do was raise his legs, try to hug him to loan him some body heat, and massage his back vigorously with what little strength he had left.

Peter's throat felt like sandpaper. Through all his efforts on the river, he'd taken only one or two sips from the water bottle in his backpack. Now he produced the precious bottle and forced Jarrad's lips apart to pour some in.

For a split-second, Jarrad's eyes fluttered open and his mouth seemed to be forming a word.

"No worries," Peter replied. Then he allowed himself a generous swallow.

"Another helicopter will come," he promised his silent companion, jerking his head up in hopefulness as the thwack of helicopter blades sounded in the distance. "This next helicopter will see us."

19 Sweet Sixteen

By the following morning, the Mount St. Helens Visitor Center had been turned into an emergency Red Cross disaster station. Chaos reigned, from ambulances, police vehicles, and a makeshift heliport outside, to long lineups of people seeking information inside. There were bedraggled survivors, weeping relatives, and weary volunteers.

Every time a helicopter arrived, people pressed forward to see if someone they knew would emerge from it—on a stretcher or walking.

Jake, Mel, and Susanna were among those who climbed out of a helicopter wearily, but with no assistance. They were ushered quickly to a room where a medic looked them over and someone else pointed them to hot coffee and sandwiches. Jake scooped up an egg-salad sandwich and stuffed it less-than-politely into his mouth.

"You're searching for other party members?" a female volunteer's voice addressed them.

"Yes, Jarrad Stopard and Peter Montpetit," Jake told the woman, who had dark circles under her eyes. She was entering their names into a computer. "Has anyone found them? Are they okay?"

"I'm checking," she replied tiredly.

"Thanks," Susanna said, her voice hoarse. It had been a long, scary night, huddled together on that point over the gully, the memory of their last glimpse of Peter and Jarrad torturing them too much to sleep. Being rescued an hour ago by helicopter had been a relief, muted by their need to know if Peter and Jarrad had been found yet, dead or alive.

"How do you spell Stopard?" the woman asked, tapping on the computer keyboard.

"One P." Jake held his breath until her fingers stopped and she looked up at them with the trace of a smile. "They were rescued by helicopter last night. They're in Toutle Hospital now, in stable condition."

"They're okay. They're okay," Susanna and Mel mumbled in trembling voices.

"They're okay," Jake echoed quietly.

"Yes. Their relatives have been informed," the worker continued. "And there are two individuals in Room C here looking for information on you. A Nancy Sheppard and Sam Miller. You know them?"

"Yes, yes!" Jake said, beginning to sprint away before he remembered his manners. "Thank you, thank you!"

"Nancy!" he shouted, flooding with emotion as he saw his lean, dark-haired boss across a sea of human beings moments later.

Nancy and Sam pushed their way through the crowd to embrace Jake and the girls.

"I'm so glad they found you," she said with tearful eyes. "We've been waiting all night for news."

Jake just nodded, speechless, as Mel and Susanna pelted Sam and Nancy with questions about Peter and Jarrad.

"We've been to the hospital," Nancy said, her hands on Jake's shoulders as she looked at him warmly.

Jake didn't mind the warm look. Why would he have ever minded Nancy's regard for him?

"They're doing okay," she continued. "Jarrad's scraped up pretty badly from logs rubbing against him in the mudflow. But he'd never have survived without Peter hanging onto him, then pulling him to shore when he got a chance. They're both in shock but doing pretty well, considering. Jarrad suffered a concussion, as I guess you already knew. They're asking about the three of you every time they wake up. And all of your parents have been phoning me. We phoned them the minute we heard you'd been found. They're on their way to meet us at our Seattle office."

"That's good," Jake said in a sleepless stupor fed by overwhelming relief.

"We're all okay," Mel said, clinging to Jake's hand. "Can you take us to the hospital?"

"If you like," Nancy said, smiling at Mel.

"Jake was the one who got us to safety," Susanna informed Sam and Nancy. "Almost got Peter and Jarrad there too. So Jake's the hero," she said with a dare-you-to-dispute-that look at Jake.

"We know. And you girls were key to everyone's survival, too. Peter filled us in on everything," Sam said, stroking his red beard thoughtfully and looking nearly as tired as Jake felt. "You can tell us your version on the way to the hospital. But you'd better phone your parents now," he added, handing over his phone.

* * *

A week later, the five mountainboarders were sitting in Sam's Seattle office, Jarrad still with ointment on his face burns, a cast on one leg where a half-submerged log had smashed against it, and bandages on both shoulders where other logs had scraped his skin raw. Peter, his knees scarred and eyes vaguely haunted, sat beside Susanna, who was clasping his hands in hers. Mel's eyes were big and serious, studying the old oak desk at which Nancy sat.

"So," Nancy began, her chair squeaking as she turned toward them with clipboard in hand. "Each of us has spoken in private several times over the past week, and it's time now to get down to business."

Jake sat quietly, shoulders hunched as he stared at the compass he'd taken from his pocket just for something to fiddle with.

Peter sat ramrod straight, his eyes on Nancy as if waiting for an execution ruling.

Jarrad, his much-signed leg cast thrust in front of him, was reading its penned signatures and messages.

Jake turned his eyes to Nancy's clipboard. The hated clipboard.

"Sam assigned Jarrad a tough job," she said, looking at each in turn. "Maybe an unfair one. Sam asked him to be objective in selecting the two best junior guides for our mountainboarding trips. He felt this was something neither he nor I should do. Neither of us mountainboard and he's friends with Mr. Michaelson. And of course both of us are fond of you boys.

"Before I tell you which two will guide the mountainboarding trips," she said, "I'd like to give you Jarrad's overall feedback. He asked me to do that before saying a few words himself."

Jake saw Jarrad shift in his seat.

"He said he was sent to teach and guide you, but instead, he learned to be guided by you."

Jake shot Jarrad a look. The man folded his big hands into his lap and kept his eyes riveted on them.

"He said he was sent to evaluate you but, in the end, learned that you were more than qualified to evaluate yourselves."

She paused. The room remained silent.

"He said he tried hard not to get to know you on a personal level because he felt that would interfere with the evaluations and final decision. But in the end, he felt honored to know you all."

Jake didn't mean to keep looking toward Jarrad, but he couldn't help it. And for a split-second, Jarrad raised his eyes to Jake. Warm, friendly eyes.

"Jarrad?" Nancy asked, lowering the clipboard. "You wanted to add something yourself?"

Jarrad nodded and straightened up in his chair. He coughed to clear his throat. "I want to apologize for being a bit rough with the evaluations," he said in a quieter voice than usual. "I thought that's the way it should be, mates." He hung his head. "I figured out I was being too harsh by the end of the week."

"If it weren't for your tough training," Jake spoke up, "we wouldn't have gotten as far as we did away from the mudflow."

Jarrad looked in surprise at Jake, then nodded slowly. "Thanks, Jake."

"And," Nancy paused to ensure she had their

attention as she sipped water from a glass on her desk, "the following is the decision he came to after talking with each of you privately and separately during your hospital visits with him."

Jake waited, throat dry, with no clear notion of what Nancy was about to say.

"First of all, he himself is resigning and returning to Australia."

Everyone's eyes swung to Jarrad in surprise. He smiled sheepishly and said, "I'm homesick. And I'm going to be the country's best one-legged mountainboarder till I'm all healed."

That brought out a few chuckles.

"It's Peter and Susanna who will continue with Sam's Adventure Tours mountainboarding trips," Nancy announced. "Melissa feels that the trip allowed her to prove her independence and abilities—to herself, her parents, and her sister—and she's realized that that is all she wanted to achieve. She feels there's no need to go on and be a guide, too. She wants to concentrate on her racing instead."

Jake, though somewhat surprised, smiled proudly at Mel, whose own smile toward him lit up her beautiful face. Both sides of her beautiful face.

"Even her parents have assured me she has fully regained her confidence and mountainboarding speed," Nancy added, smiling at Mel. "She's completed her recovery. As St. Helens will again in time," she added wistfully, glancing out the office window at majestic, snow-covered Mount Rainier.

"And Sam's Adventure Tours is sponsoring Jake in the form of a scholarship to a summer course that will earn him a special certificate in tourism studies."

Jake felt like he was lifting off his chair and flying. He was being released from a summer job he'd loved for a long time but from which he badly needed a break. Thanks to Sam and Nancy, he would be paid now to study other job options, and travel with his class while doing so. He was free—free of his former responsibilities, free of his guilt at letting Sam and Nancy down, free of his fear that quitting would end his ability to help his family. And, judging from Mel's glowing face, free from any fears that stepping down as a junior guide would cause Mel to lose respect for him.

"Of course," Nancy added, "it should go without saying that Sam and I hope Jake will return to us with his new qualifications."

Jake cocked his head and smiled at Nancy. Who could tell what the future would bring?

"As for Susanna," Nancy continued, "it also goes without saying that she rediscovered her good instincts, not that I believe she ever lost them. In letting Mel put out the log shelter's fire, she was as much a heroine as the rest of you were heroes and heroines, in my eyes."

Jake noticed Peter squeeze Susanna's hand, and Susanna hold her head high. So, she was okay with that announcement, okay with the fact that her good instincts were something to celebrate, not hide. Jake silently bet, too, that Mel no longer felt like she "owed" Susanna.

"Susanna," Nancy continued, "told me that while she started out not keen to be a guide, the nine days of training made her realize that this is what she wants to do. I must admit that this pleases me, as both Jarrad and I see her as a very responsible person."

Jake looked at Susanna to measure her reaction to that. She turned and winked at him.

"And Peter," Nancy continued, her warm eyes settling fondly on Jake's best buddy. "We are keeping him on board with his parents' full blessing. It didn't take much for Jarrad to convince them that Peter's knowledge of volcanoes is what saved the group several times over."

Jake watched Peter redden, a rare sight indeed.

"Peter also persuaded them that outdoor guiding is better leadership training than any so-called leadership course." She paused. "Anyone disagree with that?"

"Fair dinkum," Jarrad spoke up.

"No question," Susanna added.

Everyone laughed and started talking. Amid the banter, Sam exited the room and Jake rose to sit beside Melissa. She leaned toward him and placed one hand on her silver locket. "Want to know what's inside it?" she whispered playfully.

"If you're willing to show me," he replied.

She flicked it open and he stared. It was a black-and-white version of a photo he remembered Susanna snapping early on in the trip: He and Mel were grinning for the camera, faces close together. Mel was making no effort in the photo to hide one side of her face. Why should she? She was who she was, and he was crazy about her. He was also stoked, yes stoked, to be inside that locket.

"Okay with you?" she asked.

"Totally," he replied, kissing her as she snapped the locket shut.

"So," Nancy waited for the room to quiet down before lowering her clipboard and stashing it in one of the desk's drawers, "only one thing remains to be done."

Everyone gazed at her with puzzlement.

"Sam, you can come in now," she said loudly toward the closed office door.

Sam entered with an impish grin on his whiskered face, holding a tray with two cakes and a pitcher of lemonade. One cake was finished with dark chocolate frosting. The other featured white swirls of icing. Both were loaded with lit candles. Jake didn't need to count to know there were sixteen on each.

He and Peter stood, Peter actually licking his lips, as the room broke into song. "Happy birthday to you, happy birthday to you ...!"

Jarrad, using his crutches to stand, whipped his big knife out of its waist sheath and grinned. "Blow 'em out, boys, so I can cut the both of you some Aussie-sized pieces."

Jake and Peter did as they were told, Peter hurriedly claiming the chocolate cake. Jarrad carved the cakes up in no time and served the first pieces to the boys.

"Sweet sixteen," he said in his deep, gravelly voice. "And no tryin' to claim you ain't been kissed. Forget what I said about Sheilas always being trouble," he added, winking at the boys. "These two are good-o and I say good on ya! Now, if you two birthday boys don't weigh into your cake, I'm sure gonna."

"No chance," Jake said, lifting his cake out of reach. "Rack off, mate."

Jarrad laughed. Jake set his cake down, stood, and lifted his glass of lemonade.

"A toast to Sam's Adventure Tours," he declared, "and to all its guides and clients over the years ..."

"And to all the crazy things it has made us do," Peter added, jumping up and waving his glass around as the girls giggled.

"Made you do?" Nancy inserted, laughing. "Not! Anyway, better not list them or we'll be here all night."

"And finally..." Jake said, trying to think of a grand finale.

"...to Helen. The new Helen," Peter finished off for him.

"To Helen," everyone echoed approvingly, clinking their glasses with one another, then letting the cool, tart taste of lemonade slide down their throats.

Acknowledgments

Three weeks before Mount St. Helens erupted in 1980, friends and I foolishly ignored authorities and their road barriers in order to whitewater-kayak the volcano's Toutle River. The actual day of the eruption, we were caught in heavy ashfall 150 miles northeast, making it a struggle to see our way through final rapids on the Wenatchee River. I still recall pulling to shore, turning my boat over, and soberly writing my name on it in the ash that fell as everyone thronged around car radios, shocked at the news. Mount St. Helens, it turned out, had erupted much sooner and more violently than anyone had predicted. Had my Toutle and Wenatchee weekends been swapped around, it's unlikely I'd be alive today.

Tragically, the eruption killed at least fifty-seven people and injured many others—most of them well outside the restricted zones and unaware they were taking any risk. The eruption also destroyed countless wildlife, trees, and property. And yet, scientists have been impressed by the rate of St. Helens's recovery. Certainly, the eruption's contribution to scientific knowledge has been invaluable, directly saving many lives in volcanic eruptions since.

Special thanks to friends from Naples, Italy, who

walked my husband and me through Pompeii last year: Marco, Marta, and Marisa Moracci. Pompeii is the city that was buried for two thousand years when nearby Mount Vesuvius erupted in A.D. 79. Hundreds of skeletons were excavated near the beach, where people waited frantically for rescue by boat, or sought cover from the raining pumice under stone arches. Most were suffocated by hot clouds of ash. Boats in the harbor fared little better, being pummeled by red-hot chunks of pumice for seven hours.

Luckily, an eyewitness across the bay—"Pliny the Younger"—left a detailed account that is helpful to this day. Ever since then, super-explosive eruptions like that of Vesuvius and Mount St. Helens have been called "Plinian" eruptions.

Another interesting fact: Naples, Italy, suffered extensive damage during the Second World War because even though residents attempted blackouts at night—turning off outdoor lights and darkening their windows—bombers flying over the city could always identify where the city lay by the glow in Vesuvius's crater.

As for the mountainboarding aspect of the plot, I am indebted to three Australian mountainboarders who hosted me during a visit to Melbourne, Australia. They helped contribute ideas and answered my many questions about the sport. These include instructor and event organizer John Morton, competitor Jarrad Cronin, and boarder/videographer "Gog."

John Morton in particular exchanged countless e-mails with me and read more than one version of the manuscript. John is not only a tireless promoter of the sport, he is also author of the informational website www.mfrworks.com.au/frameworX.

I was also honored to have Daniel Dworkin read through and tweak the manuscript. Daniel is a teacher in San Francisco, as well as a mountainboarder and mountainboard race organizer.

Dr. Martin Blackwell, G.P., vetted all medical aspects of the manuscript.

Rosaly M. C. Lopes read the entire manuscript to review material regarding volcanoes; she's an author and award-winning scientist with expertise in lava flows who works with the NASA Jet Propulsion Laboratory at the California Institute of Technology.

My teen editor, Julian Legere, and my husband, Steve Withers, also offered valuable feedback.

Among the literature I read on volcanoes, I'd like to acknowledge *Mount St. Helens: The Eruption and Recovery of a Volcano* by Rob Carson (Sasquatch Books, 1990); *Echoes of Fury: The 1980 Eruption of Mount St. Helens and the Lives It Changed Forever* by Frank Parchman (Epicenter Press, 2005); *Surviving Galleras* by Stanley Williams and Fen Montaigne (Houghton

Mifflin Company, 2001); and *The Volcano Adventure Guide* by Rosaly Lopes (Cambridge University Press, 2005).

Naturally, I'd like to thank my editor, Carolyn Bateman; my literary agent, Leona Trainer; my speaking tours agent, Chris Patrick; and all the staff of Whitecap and Firefly Books.

Close to eight years ago, Leona and Whitecap Books both took a big risk when they decided to publish my first novel, *Raging River.* It has been an exciting and successful ride since—for all of us, I hope. May the publishing field remain open to new writers!

And last but not least, I need to thank all my readers, without whom Jake and Peter would never have enjoyed so many adventures. This is the tenth and final book in the Take It to the Xtreme series. (The books need not be read in order.) But stay tuned for many adventure novels yet to come, or e-mail me your comments and ideas through my website: www.TakeItToTheExtreme.com.

1

ISBN 978-1-55285-510-2

"Up shot the kayak into the air, only to perform a harrowing backflip. Shoved helmet-first into the center of the spinning cocoon, Peter had never felt a force so determined to pry him from his boat. Hanging upside down, gripping his paddle shaft with all his might, Peter waited, counted, and prayed."

Arch rivals and sometimes friends Peter and Jake are delighted to be part of a whitewater-rafting trip. But after a series of disasters leaves the group stranded in the wilderness, it's up to them to confront the dangerous rapids to search for help. This is the first title in the Take It to the Xtreme series by Pam Withers.

2

Jake, Peter, and Moses are looking forward to heli-skiing and snowboarding in the backcountry near Whistler. But just after they're dropped off on a mountain peak, bad weather closes in and a helicopter crashes. It's up to them to rescue any survivors and overcome avalanches, hypothermia, and wild animals to make their way to safety. This is the second title in the Take It to the Xtreme series.

ISBN 978-1-55285-530-0

It's summer vacation for best friends Peter and Jake, and when they're invited to help develop a mountain-bike trail west of the Canadian Rockies, they can't believe their luck. But as they start working hard in an isolated park, the boys sense that something's not right. Join the boys as they plunge into the mountain-biking descent of their lives.

3

ISBN 978-1-55285-604-8

Fifteen-year-olds Jake and Peter land jobs as skateboarding stuntboys on a movie set. The boys couldn't be happier, but their dream job proves to be more trouble than they expected. A demanding director, an uneasy relationship with three local skateboarding toughs, and a sabotage attempt—which suggests a jealous rival in their midst—are just some of the obstacles these stuntboys encounter. Coaching from the town's new skate park manager—a former X-Games champ—helps. But after a police chase and an accident that lands someone in the hospital, Jake and Peter know it's time to find out who has it in for them, and why!

ISBN 978-1-55285-647-5

4

Jake and Peter find extreme adventure once again. This time a scuba-diving accident leaves the best friends and a surfer girl stranded on a deserted island with surfboards as their only means of escape. The storm of the century is fast approaching, and the boys need to think fast if they're going to get home in one piece. *Surf Zone* is Jake and Peter's most action-packed, thrilling adventure yet. This book is sure to keep readers on the edge of their seats.

ISBN 978-1-55285-718-2

5

6

ISBN 978-1-55285-783-0

Jake and Peter stumble upon adrenalin-pumping adventure yet again, this time high in the peaks of the Bugaboo Mountains, just west of the Canadian Rockies. Jake is obsessed with solo-climbing a soaring granite spire. His best friend Peter is as absorbed with filming Jake for a video as he is in not divulging his secret fear of heights to the runaway girl who joins them.

Packed with mountaineering lore and cliff-hanging tension, *Vertical Limits,* the sixth in the Take It to the Xtreme series, has competitive gym climbing, outdoor urban climbing, and wilderness rock climbing.

7

Jake and Peter spend the summer as junior guides for a dirt-bike trail outfitter on a remote ranch near Spokane, Washington. They consider themselves the ideal team, but Peter is a freestyle maniac who hates doing bike maintenance and Jake dreams of being a motocross-race mechanic. It takes a series of race mishaps topped off by a natural disaster to convince them that successful dirt bikers understand their motorcycles inside and out.

ISBN 978-1-55285-804-2

8

Jake and Peter are junior instructors at a noisy wakeboard school that's attempting to share a remote lake with a community of "save-the-earth society dropouts" (otherwise known as hippies.). When Peter decides to encourage the wild streak in a rebellious hippie girl across the lake, she runs away to hide in a nearby abandoned sawmill, only to discover it's not as abandoned as it looks. Soon, community tensions erupt, and the boys get more action than they bargained for.

ISBN 978-1-55285-856-1

9

ISBN 978-1-55285-904-9

In between racing and dirt-jumping their BMX bikes, daredevil fifteen-year-olds Jake and Peter discover an astounding underground maze of old mining tunnels. Equipped with night-vision goggles, they get drawn into riding underground—defying a group of hostile riders and surviving unexpected tremors. As they attempt to race their bikes against time back up to daylight, Peter must come to terms with personal misfortunes threatening to suffocate all that he has come to think of as normal.